SORRY
I'M NOT SORRY

Published in Nashville, Tennessee, by Tommy Nelson. Tommy Nelson is
an imprint of Thomas Nelson. Thomas Nelson is a registered trademark of
HarperCollins Christian Publishing, Inc.

Tommy Nelson titles may be purchased in bulk for educational, business,
fund-raising, or sales promotional use. For information, please e-mail
SpecialMarkets@ThomasNelson.com.

Library of Congress Cataloging-in-Publication Data

Rue, Nancy N.
Sorry I'm not sorry / Nancy Rue.
pages cm -- (Mean girl makeover ; book 3)
Summary: While in mandatory counseling to avoid being expelled from Gold
Country Middle School for bullying, Kilie Steppe, twelve, focuses on getting
revenge against Tory, who took her place as "queen bee," while revealing details
that might explain why she preys on her peers.
ISBN 978-1-4003-2372-2 (paperback)
[1. Bullies--Fiction. 2. Counseling--Fiction. 3. Tutors and tutoring--Fiction.
4. Conduct of life--Fiction. 5. Middle schools--Fiction. 6. Schools--Fiction. 7.
Family problems--Fiction.] I. Title. II. Title: Sorry I am not sorry.
PZ7.R88515Sp 2015
[Fic]--dc23
    2014047636

Printed in the United States of America

15 16 17 18 19 US 5 4 3 2 1

SORRY I'M NOT SORRY

MEAN GIRL MAKEOVER

BOOK 3

By
NANCY RUE

THOMAS NELSON
Since 1798

NASHVILLE   MEXICO CITY   RIO DE JANEIRO

Chapter One

The story I'm about to tell you is totally true, and it started the summer the G.G.s—the Goody-Goodies—took everything away from me.

I didn't think they could do that. I didn't think anybody could. So when my mom and my dad and I walked up the steps of Gold Country Middle School that morning in June, I wasn't even nervous. Some twelve-year-old girls would've been munching on their fingernails or making breakfast out of the ends of their hair, but not me.

My just-trimmed-yesterday bob was swinging in the Grass Valley breeze.

My armpits under my pink-striped tee were powder dry.

And my mind was so calm I was practically asleep.

The only irritableness was coming from my father. He took off his sunglasses and looked down at my mom and said, "I told the woman there was no need for a face-to-face meeting."

The "woman" he was talking about was the principal, Mrs. Yeats. I called her the Chin Freak. Not to her face, of course. Even *I* couldn't get away with that.

Mom tossed her straight dark hair—like mine only longer—out of her face and waited for Dad to open one of the doors while she thumbed her cell phone. "It's either this or Kylie doesn't get back in, so humor her."

Dad said something about that not being our only option. He was always talking about options and other boring lawyer things, but in this case, I was okay with it because it probably meant he was going to fix what he called This Situation before Mrs. Yeats could wiggle her chins too many times.

I switched to noticing how weird it was to be at Gold Country Middle when there was no school going on. No Patrick and Andrew and Douglas hanging out on the steps, making comments that sounded rude but really just meant they liked me. Especially Douglas. No signs on the door announcing all the stuff that made school worth coming to. Like dances and cheerleading tryouts.

The strangest part? My posse wasn't standing as usual by the trophy case across from the office waiting for me to start the day. Riannon. Heidi. Izzy.

Actually, Riannon and Heidi *were* there, but it wasn't "as usual." Their parents were there too. It didn't *get* much more bizarre than that. Both of their moms were talking with their hands flapping all around and their gel nails reflecting off the glass on the case, and the dads had their arms folded across their stiff white shirts and foreheads scrunched practically down to their noses.

As for Riannon and Heidi, although they were flattened against the glass like they were trying to become part of it, when they saw me, their faces sprang into action and we had one of those conversations only best friends can have—the kind where you don't actually say a word.

Heidi's hazel eyes bugged, sort of like a pug dog. Translation: *This isn't turning out the way we planned.*

Riannon darted her green ones to her mother, whose voice was now sounding like Minnie Mouse's, and zippered her finger across her lips. Translation: *I can't talk in front of her.*

I rolled my eyes and held up both of my thumbs and twitched them. Translation: *Text me.*

"Not going to happen, Kylie," Minnie—uh, Riannon's mom—said. She curled her long fingers around Riannon's bare arm and peeled her away from the trophy case. "Riannon won't be texting you. E-mailing you. Or calling you. We're done."

She gave a nod like a punctuation mark and dragged Riannon to the door where her dad was already waiting. Somehow Heidi had also been hauled away, and when the big door shut, all the air was sucked out of the hallway.

I recovered fast, though. My parents had already disappeared inside the office, which gave me a minute to laugh. Was Riannon's mom a crazy person? Of *course* Riannon was going to find a way to text me, even if she had to wait until her mom got over herself and forgot about it. Which she always did.

All our moms did.

Mine poked her head out of the office door then and said, "Hello? Let's get this over with."

That was the thing that made my mom different from Riannon's and Heidi's: she never sounded like Minnie or any other mouse. She was more like a mama panther.

So I sailed past the secretary's empty desk and followed Mom into Mrs. Yeats' office. The last time I stood before the Chin Freak, I'd pretty much had a screaming meltdown. This time, though, I was ready for her. I was going to be totally cool because, like my mom said, we were just there to humor her. I could do humorous. I could do cooperative. I could do irresistible.

I could do anything.

Until I saw who *else* was in Mrs. Yeats' office, sitting in front of her desk like they were members of the *faculty*. It was two of the three people I most wished would break out in acne.

One was Ginger Hollingberry, better known to my posse and me as "Gingerbread"—and not in a good way. She was the freckly, red-haired annoyance of a person who started the whole hot mess to begin with.

The other was the Dwarf. Lydia Somebody. She was a weirdly short woman with too much hair who thought she could come in and stop it all.

I'm scared.

I froze in the doorway, not because of Gingerbread and the Dwarf, but because I hadn't heard that tiny voice in a long time. It was a wee thing inside my head that nobody knew about but me. Now was not the time for it to be whispering and definitely not the time for me to start listening to it.

"Kylie," Mrs. Yeats said. "Come join us."

All of her chins were wiggling, so at least I had something else to think about as I plopped down in a chair next to my mom. The first time we met with the principal, Mom wondered on the way home why the woman didn't have plastic surgery.

"Mr. Steppe?" Mrs. Yeats said as she motioned Dad toward the last empty seat.

"I'm fine back here." Dad sounded like we were about to watch a movie or something. I couldn't see him, but I could hear the bright smile in his voice. Dad's teeth were always as white as Tic Tacs.

Mrs. Yeats folded her hands at her thick waist. Just like every other day she wore a gold vest with all these buttons and pins on it that said stuff like, *Go Miners!* and *Miners Make Good Citizens* and a new one, *Bullying Is Everybody's Problem.* Lydia must have given her that one.

"It's my job to determine," Mrs. Yeats was saying as she nodded her head of gray hair that looked like a space helmet, "whether to recommend that Kylie be readmitted to Gold Country Middle for the next school year."

"And you've decided?" Dad said.

"I have not. Certain criteria will have to be met before I can make that determination." Mrs. Yeats looked at me with eyes that were probably meant to make me break out in hives, which I didn't. "You know what *criteria* are, Kylie?"

Did she think I was an idiot? I was in honors classes.

"The things you're going to make me do," I said. I tried to smile like Dad.

"Wrong."

What? I always aced vocabulary.

"I'm not going to *make* you do anything. This is going to be your choice, and I want it to be a genuine one."

She waited like she expected me to say something. Maybe that was the first "criteria." So I said in my I-am-cooperative voice, "What do you want me to choose to do?"

Out of the corner of my eye, I thought I saw Lydia pass her hand over her mouth, like she was wiping off a smile. I didn't turn my head, though. I really didn't like to look at her.

"The first one may be the hardest," Mrs. Yeats said. "I want to see you apologize to Ginger."

My mom's face came up from her phone. "For?"

Mrs. Yeats answered like *I* was the one who asked. "For all the things you've done to make Ginger's time here miserable. Do you want me to list them?"

I had to work really hard not to roll my eyes, which my mom had told me on the way over I better not do. But really? I'd heard "the list" so many times I could recite it like the Pledge of Allegiance.

Still, I was kind of knocked sideways. If somebody had *told* me I was going to have to make an apology, I would have rehearsed it. Good thing this was Gingerbread we were talking about. She was *so* easy to mess with.

I got up and went to Ginger and leaned against the front of Mrs. Yeats' desk. Ginger looked up at me, and I realized how blue her eyes were. I'd never noticed that before. The one time she had actually looked at me long enough I was too mad to notice that she even *had* eyes.

But now I talked right into them.

"Aw, Ginger," I said. "I'm sorry things got blown out of proportion." I tilted my head so my hair splashed against the side of my face. "At first we were just playing around, and then everybody took it so seriously and—" I sighed like my mom did when she didn't want to keep explaining why I couldn't wear high heels yet. "I'm just really sorry it ended up like this. Are we okay?"

I expected her to jump up and try to hug me and say, "I'm sorry too!" Even though I was glad she didn't, I was surprised. She didn't even answer my question. She just looked at me with her really blue eyes until I had to fight not to be the first one to look away.

"Ginger," Mrs. Yeats said, massaging the chins. "Are you satisfied with that apology?"

She sounded like she didn't see how anybody *could* be, but Ginger nodded.

"You believe it was genuine?" Mrs. Yeats said.

"I don't mean to be critical," Dad said, "but I think you might be leading the witness a little bit."

6

That was probably lawyer talk too. Maybe I needed to learn some of that.

Before Mrs. Yeats could say anything, Ginger nodded again and said, "I believe she believes everything she said."

Huh?

While I was trying to untangle that, Mrs. Yeats told Ginger she could go, which she did without even glancing my way.

Mom dropped her phone into her purse. "Kylie apologized. The girl accepted. Are we good?"

"'I'm sorry' doesn't solve the problem."

I jerked without meaning to. I guess I'd just forgotten how . . . different Lydia's voice was. It was almost the way people sound when they breathe in balloon gas. It was weird how people could think she was so wise or whatever when she talked like that, but everybody else seemed to.

Lydia looked at me. *Her* eyes were dark and snappy, and she had stared into me with them before. I didn't like it then either.

"You don't really take any responsibility for what happened to Ginger that night, do you?" she said.

"I have to intervene here," Dad said.

I was still leaning against Mrs. Yeats' desk, so I could see him going into what my sister called Counselor for the Defense mode. I didn't much care for it when he went there with me, but I was digging it at the moment. *This* was what was supposed to happen.

"Just to be clear," Dad said, still flashing his teeth, "Kylie didn't do any physical harm to—what's our girl's name?"

"'Our' girl's name is Ginger Hollingberry.'" Lydia's balloon voice was calm. "And she sustained a broken rib, among other things."

"But Kylie wasn't there at the time. Isn't that correct?"

Go get 'em, Dad.

But Mrs. Yeats put up her hand. The chins were now very still. "We've been through all of this before, people. Let's move forward."

Dad spread out both hands. "Let's do."

"Based on that apology, I am not inclined to recommend that Kylie be reinstated as a student here."

But if I'd had time to rehearse—

"However, there are additional criteria, and after those are met, perhaps we can revisit this."

There you go. I would have time to practice a better "apology." And if that was the hardest part, like she said, how bad could the rest of it be?

"Before you go any further," Dad said, "because I don't want you to go to a lot of trouble over something that may turn out to be a moot point . . ."

I had no idea what that was, but I was sure I was going to like it.

"I should tell you," Dad went on, "that we're looking into private school for Kylie for next year."

"And how's that working out for you, Mr. Steppe?"

I flash-froze again, just like I had in the doorway. Only this time it was *all* because of the wee voice that said . . .

This is so humiliating, I wish I could evaporate.

Dad had already tried to get me into private schools. Three of them. And they all said I had the grades and test scores, but they wouldn't take me because of my conduct record. The record that was perfect until Tori and Ginger and the rest of the G.G.s.

"What are these 'criteria' or whatever?" Mom drummed her fingers on her crossed arms. She wasn't as good at pretending to be patient as my dad.

"I have them written out for you." Mrs. Yeats picked up some papers from her desk behind us. "Kylie, if you'll have a seat, I'll go over them."

"Seriously? I think we can read this for ourselves—"

Mrs. Yeats clipped off Mom's words and sliced right on. There were moments when I would have enjoyed that. This wasn't one of them because as Mrs. Yeats went down the sheet, each "criteria" got more evil than the one before it.

Bad: I had to do 120 hours of community service to show that I could care about other people.

Worse: I had to work with a tutor to make up a project to pass social studies because Mr. Jett said my performance up until I was expelled didn't satisfy the requirement.

The worst thing ever: I had to work with Lydia Kiriakos on my "bullying behavior," and she was also the social studies tutor Mrs. Yeats had approved.

By that time, I almost didn't care whether I got back into her stupid school. Only one thing held me back from throwing a level-five tantrum.

"After I do all this," I said, "I'm reinstituted."

"Reinstated."

What*ever!*

"I'll be back on the cheerleading squad too. That's true, right?"

The answer was the only thing worth holding my breath for, and I did. Mrs. Yeats waited so long to give it, I was ready to pass out.

"That will be up to Mrs. Bernstein," she said, just as I was turning blue. "She's the advisor, so it's her choice."

All the air I'd been holding drained out like *I* was the balloon full of helium. Mrs. Bernstein and I used to be almost like friends, if you could be friends with a teacher, but the G.G.s had even gotten to her, and I was pretty sure she didn't like me anymore.

I don't think anybody likes me anymore.

I launched away from Mrs. Yeats' desk and headed for the door, flinging words over my shoulder. "I'm going to the car."

Stay mad, I told myself as I dodged the desks in the office and made it to the hall. That was the only way—stay mad.

At Mr. Jett for failing me when I used to be his favorite student.

At Mrs. Bernstein for dropping me—and my posse—from the squad so I couldn't go to cheerleading camp, which I'd been living for the entire year.

At Mrs. Yeats and the Dwarf and all the other adults who decided that being popular meant you were a bully.

I stopped at the corner of the hallway and looked for something to smack or kick or tear down. I searched the wall, but it was poster-less. Except for one.

There it was. The perfect thing.

My eyes squinted down so far I could barely see it, really, but it was there. Big as a pep rally poster and full of sixth graders' signatures. Mine was on it but only because I didn't want to work with her—Lydia—and that's what happened when you wouldn't sign. A lot of good that did me.

I chewed on the inside of my cheek. I hated that poster, that Code. Not because of what it said. I didn't even *know* what it said, and I didn't care. All I knew was that because of it, Tori Taylor and her G.G.s had taken everything away from me. And she was the third person I wished would look in the mirror one morning and find out she had incurable acne.

I reached up to the top of the poster and pulled part of it away from the wall so I could get my fingers behind it. One yank and it would rip in half.

But just then my cell vibrated in my pocket. Probably Riannon. I could find out if they'd given her all those criteria thingies too, and we could make a plan to get rid of them. I let go of the poster and dug out my phone.

It wasn't Riannon texting me. It was Izzy, who right now would be like a mosquito buzzing around my head. I poised my thumbs to start a message to Ri, and suddenly other thumbs were grabbing my phone from me.

"Da-ad!"

"Sorry, princess," he said, stuffing it into his pants pocket. "No phone and no Internet for a while."

I changed tactics. "Mo-om!"

"Don't look at me," she said and teetered on her heels as she followed Dad toward the door.

"I don't get it!"

They didn't stop walking away from me even after we got out of the front door and the sun hit us square in the face. Mom just pulled her sunglasses from the top of her head and stayed on Dad's trail to our white SUV parked at the curb by a sign marked Buses Only.

Dad opened the back door and tapped my nose with his finger like he always did when he was trying to make me do something. "I want you to stay out of trouble until I can get you into the Roseville School."

"You already talked to the people at Roseville," Mom said.

"I'm not done with them," Dad said. To me, he said, "I don't agree with this whole thing, princess, but you're going to have to work with it for now."

"But Daddy—"

He shook his head and I climbed into the backseat, but as soon as he got behind the wheel again, I started back in.

"This is so unfair. It wasn't all my fault."

"Other people don't see it that way. You're going to have to play the game for a while."

"I don't want to play the game."

Mom's hair flipped toward me, and when her face caught up, it was sharp and shut-up pointy. "Do you want to be a cheerleader or not?"

I shut up.

But only for a minute. As we were pulling onto our street, I said, "You're getting somebody else to tutor me, though, right? Somebody besides that Lydia person?"

"We're stuck with her." Mom turned back around. "But the good news is that she's coming to *our* house two afternoons a week. That way I can be around to make sure she's not brainwashing you or something."

You're going to be around? Really?

I want that.

This time I didn't shut down my wee voice because I wanted that too.

Chapter Two

I stalked straight to my room when we got home. Actually, not my real room. Our ancient house on Church Street was being remodeled, and my actual bedroom was all bare floor and freaky wallboards right then, so I had to share Jocelyn's room until mine was done. That was fine because she was my favorite person in the family. I didn't tell her that because that would've been, like, *awk*ward, but she was eighteen and cool and took me places in her car.

She wasn't there when I flounced in and slammed the door. She was almost never there because she took *other* people places in her car too. It was a BMW convertible, and she said her friends liked being seen in it. Who wouldn't, right? I kind of wished she *was* there so I could vent (she called it a Drama Dump), but since she wasn't, I had the perfect opportunity to get on her computer and e-mail Heidi and Riannon. Jocelyn probably wouldn't have stopped me anyway.

The first thing I did, though, was look under the king-size bed for Margaret.

"Kitty, kitty?" I said in my part-meow-part-purr-part-me voice. "Kylie's home."

She answered with her usual meow-purr-Margaret for *finally*!

She crawled to me and straight into my lap, all-black and fluffy except for the one white front paw that looked like it had been dipped in whipped cream. She must have thought it had been, too, because she was always licking it. Right now she patted my face with it and searched my eyes with her wide yellow ones. This is going to sound wacko, but sometimes when she looked at me like that, I knew she was saying, *Where were you? What did you do? Who did you see? Did they like you?*

Maybe it was because those were the questions—except for that last one—my first Margaret used to ask me when I came home from school every day. But she wasn't a cat. She was my nanny from England who was with me from the time I was born until third grade. Kitty Margaret came when my parents decided I didn't need a nanny anymore, and my first Margaret went back to London, and I pitched a fit that went into the Tantrum Hall of Fame. Although I got attached to my kitten right away, she never totally took my nanny's place. She couldn't call me wee thing and say how much she loved to hear me talk in my wee voice.

After she left, I never talked that way again except to my cat. But sometimes that voice tried to talk to me in my head, and that freaked me out. I never let the wee voice speak for long.

I carried Margaret to Jocelyn's desk in a little study alcove thing that was part of her suite. Jocelyn told me she didn't see why my parents put that in there since she was going to San Francisco for college at the end of the summer, but right now it was perfect. You couldn't see it from the door, so if Mom came in, she wouldn't catch me on the computer. If she did, I'd say I was getting a head start on research for the project I had to do for social studies. It was always good to have a backup plan.

I emailed Heidi and Riannon both at once and told them everything about what happened in Mrs. Yeats' office, only I left out the part where I noticed Ginger's blue eyes—what was that even about, anyway?—and how I lost the stare-down with her. It was a freak accident, so why go there?

Then I did my questions:

What did the Chin Freak say to you? Do you have to do all the hours of working in the slums with homeless people or whatever? (Like she could really make me do that! Like my dad would even let me!) Did you pass Mr. Traitor Jett's class? Do you have to work with the Dwarf too? This is all about that Code thing, and now they're going to make us follow it, or we don't get to do anything. I can't believe this is happening, but we'll find a way to stop it. Come for a sleepover tomorrow night, and we'll make a plan.

I hit Send and scratched between Margaret's velvety ears, just the way she liked it. I should hear from Riannon in about five minutes because now that she had an iPad, she practically slept with it, which was good because sometimes after Jocelyn and I stayed up late watching movies, I liked to chat with Riannon online when I couldn't fall asleep.

Heidi usually took longer because she never sat still long enough to stay on her phone or her computer. She had ADHD or something like that. My mom always referred to her as Hyper Heidi. Jocelyn said she acted like she had to go to the bathroom all the time.

After half an hour without a ding from Jocelyn's computer, *I* was getting hyper. I checked it about twelve times, and when there was no answer from either of them, I set Margaret in a splash of sun on the windowsill and went into a split on the shrimp-colored carpet. I always thought better when I was doing some moves.

In the split . . . maybe Minnie Mouse was actually watching Riannon, and it would be tomorrow before she gave in and Ri could get back to me.

Doing forward rolls . . . Heidi could be at the mall. Her mom always bought her something when she was sulking, and nobody could pout like Heidi. She could make her bottom lip look like a fold-out couch.

Getting into a headstand . . . I could call Izzy. She and her parents didn't have a meeting with Mrs. Yeats because she wasn't as "involved in the bullying" as the rest of us. She only got suspended and lost her cheerleading privileges. But she might still know what was going on because Izzy was like this miniature dachshund we used to have: even though she was kind of round, she could burrow into small places and find stuff without anybody seeing her. The problem was that then she would bark it to everybody and we'd be like, "Izzy! Shut up!" I couldn't handle her right now.

As I tried to decide whether there was enough room in Jocelyn's suite for a cartwheel, I thought of Shelby. She used to be in our posse before she turned on us. Shelby was kind of the nice one, and that was good sometimes, but it backfired. Now if one of us even looked at her, her mother would be in Mrs. Yeats' office and we'd be . . .

Suspended? Expelled? That happened anyway even without Shelby. That was too bad because I could've used a little bit of nice. When was Jocelyn coming home?

I'm lonely.

I decided I could do a cartwheel. I did three of them.

∾

By the next day, Saturday, I still hadn't heard from Heidi or Riannon. I didn't even go outside to our pool or watch a movie in our home theater or bug Mom to take *me* to the mall in Sacramento, since there wasn't a decent place to shop in dinky Grass Valley or Nevada City. Mom wasn't home anyway. It was her birthday, and she and Dad were playing golf at Alta Sierra Country Club. I spent the whole day in Jocelyn's suite, close to the computer. Still nothing.

"Okay," Jocelyn said at five o'clock that afternoon. "Enough with the gymnastics in here." She stood in the doorway of the walk-in closet with a slithery-looking silver tank top on a hanger in one hand and a pink thing with a tangle of straps in the other. "Which one for tonight?"

I sprawled on the floor next to Margaret and shrugged one shoulder. "You look good in both of them."

That was totally true. Jocelyn was tall and flowy like a ballerina—although she gave up dance when she was fourteen because it was boring—and she had shoulder-length silky hair, blonde like Dad's was before his started to go silver. If she didn't look good in an outfit, it was the outfit's fault.

I was totally different from her, so different some people didn't even believe we were sisters. I was one of the shortest kids in our class, and my hair was dark like Mom's was before she put blonde streaks in it. Jocelyn's eyes were green, though not the fake color from contact lenses like Riannon's, and mine were blue with gold flecks in them. My nanny Margaret used to say they were magic eyes.

I shook back my hair. Why was I thinking about her so much all of a sudden?

"You're a huge help, Ky. Thanks." Jocelyn started to go back into the closet, but she stopped and narrowed her eyes down into green dashes. "What's up with you, anyway? You're acting all weird."

Finally, somebody actually asked. I sat up so fast that Margaret complained and scooted under the bowl chair where Jocelyn threw all her clothes.

"I need a Drama Dump."

"Ya think?"

She was headed for the bed and so was I when there was a knock on the door, and it opened before Jocelyn could say, "Go away!" Dad's blonde-gray head appeared.

"Sure, come on in," Jocelyn said.

Her voice was all drippy with sarcasm, but it was like Dad didn't even hear it. He never did when he had that look on his face—the one that said, *Here's what we're doing now.*

"Get dressed, you two," he said. "We're taking your mother to dinner."

"I already have plans," Jocelyn said.

"You can't postpone them? For your mother's birthday?"

Jocelyn opened her mouth, but he was already backing out the door.

"Where are we going?" I called to him. I really didn't care except that it might be a place where I could run into Heidi or Riannon. They were always going out to eat with their parents.

"The Owl," he called back.

When his footsteps had faded down the stairs, Jocelyn and I looked at each other.

"I hate the Owl," we both said.

∾

The only thing that made leaving the house worth it was that as we were getting into the car, the guy who was doing the remodeling was packing up his stuff to leave too, and Dad got all over him—in his Counsel for the Defense way—about some paint that got sprayed on a rose bush. Why did that make me smile into my hand?

Because the guy was Ginger's father.

Beside me in the backseat, Jocelyn got kind of stiff. "I wish Dad wouldn't do that," she said, like she wasn't really talking to anybody.

"Why?" I whispered.

"Because of that thing with the van," she whispered back.

I kept an eye on Mom and Dad as they stood over Mr. Hollingberry. "He's never going to do anything about that. They're poor. He won't make Dad mad and get fired."

"Yeah, well, I hope not." Jocelyn nudged my leg with hers. "Shh. Here they come."

Too bad because I had a question: *Why didn't Dad fire Ginger's dad after Ginger made all this trouble for me?*

That thought only just occurred to me, and it made me chew the inside of my cheek.

∿

The Owl Grill was just as bad as it was the last time we were in there. It was dark and old-fashioned like everything else in Grass Valley, like we were still living in the gold mining days instead of the twenty-first century, and they had stuff on the menu like deep-fried Brussels sprouts. Who eats that?

Maybe it was worse because I was in a bad mood. For one thing, everybody got to be on their phones but me. Mom got a text from somebody, so she answered over the calamari, which I hate because of those icky suction cup things. Dad had a phone call just as the salads were arriving, so he stepped out. I was so annoyed with him, I forgot to tell the waiter when to stop grinding the pepper over mine, so I couldn't eat it. And Jocelyn was on Facebook the whole time, trying to rearrange meeting up with her friends later. That made me even madder about the sleepover that wasn't happening. My thumbs kept twitching as I watched all of them.

Not only that, but when my mom finally did put down her phone to eat her shrimp, she stopped with her fork halfway to her mouth and looked at me like I had just shown up that minute. "Why did you wear *that* top?" she said.

I looked down at my lacy white cami. "Because I wanted to," I said.

"White is never a good choice for you. I can see the black cat hair on it from here."

Jocelyn looked up from the steak she wasn't eating. "Mother, it's too dark in here to see the cat herself if she traipsed across the table."

I kind of liked the thought of Margaret walking through the short ribs my dad was having and leaving barbecue sauce paw prints on the tablecloth.

"It's too small anyway," Mom went on. "It pulls across your—"

"Mo-om!" I said between my teeth.

"It does, and it looks tacky."

"Ohmygosh, Kylie," Jocelyn said, her eyes popping like a cartoon character. "How could you even think about leaving the house looking tacky?"

Her poppy eyes told me what to do.

"I know, right?" I said.

"Clearly, there can be no tacky emerging from the Steppe mansion."

"You're not funny," Mom said.

I thought she was.

"I have a scathingly brilliant idea," Jocelyn said. "If her clothes are too small, why don't you take her shopping? Wait, never mind. I will."

"Uh-oh," Dad said. "What are you using for money?"

Jocelyn smiled like a beauty pageant winner. "Your credit card, Daddy."

Dad pretended to groan. "I knew this conversation was going to cost me."

I looked at Mom to see what *she* was going to say, but she was on her phone again.

The waiter came back to our table then, and I wondered if he had been waiting for the argument that didn't really sound like an argument to be over.

"May I take some of these dishes away for you?" he asked.

"Yes," Dad said without looking at him.

"And our water glasses are empty," Mom said. "Again."

"I'll take care of that right away," the waiter said.

"And would you wipe my mother's mouth for her when you come back?" Jocelyn muttered.

I started to laugh, but she squeezed my leg. It wouldn't have mattered because my parents were both on their phones *again*.

"Ah," Dad said. "This is what I was waiting for." He tapped his screen. "E-mail from the headmaster at the Roseville School. Good news, princess. He and I are having lunch next week."

"What if I don't want to go there?" I hadn't planned to say that, but the words just burst out on their own.

Dad had dark eyebrows—just the way Jocelyn did even though they were both blondes—and he was always doing things with them. Right now he turned them into a squiggly line.

"Why wouldn't you want to go there? It's the best school within a hundred-mile radius." The squiggly line flattened into a straight one. "I don't know why we didn't send you there in the first place."

"You know why," Mom said. "Their athletic program is pathetic."

Dad painted on a smile for me. "Since when were you an athlete? You quit soccer when you were, what, five?"

"They don't have cheerleading!"

It was one of those moments in a crowded place when until then everybody is talking. But just at the second you blurt out something, the whole room had gone silent the second before, and everybody hears you and everybody stares like a naked person just walked in.

"Anyone care for dessert?" the waiter said.

Jocelyn nudged me off my chair. "You two have a crème brûlée or something. I'm taking Kylie down to the Lazy Dog for ice cream."

She smiled at the waiter and said, "Good luck," and ushered me out the front door.

"That went well," she said when we were headed down Mill Street. Even in the almost-dark, I could see that her face was hard. "Reason Number Five Hundred and Twelve why I can't wait to leave for college. "

Don't go . . . please don't go.

"Do you think if I have a double sundae, it'll make me fat?" I said.

"Don't even start with me, Kylie," she said.

Chapter Three

Jocelyn and I went shopping at the Arden Fair Mall in Sacramento the next day, Sunday, and we took Izzy with us. Heidi and Riannon still hadn't answered my e-mail, and I couldn't stand not knowing what was going on for another minute.

"Tell me again why we're bringing Motor Mouth?" Jocelyn said when we were waiting for Izzy to get to the car.

"I need to talk to her," I said.

"Good luck getting a word in," she said.

When Izzy climbed into the tiny backseat of Jocelyn's car, it was like she pushed her Power button at the same time.

"I'm so jazzed I get to ride in a Beamer! This is the coolest car ever! I want one like this when I get my license. Either this or a Camaro. Or a Ford F-150."

"So you can either haul tail or haul stuff," Jocelyn said into the rearview mirror.

"I was hoping you'd have the top down," Izzy babbled on, like Jocelyn hadn't even said anything. "I've never ridden in a convertible with the top down. Okay, I did ride in my uncle's Gator, but that's not like an actual car . . ."

As Izzy continued to jack her jaws, Jocelyn leaned her head toward me and said, "When do we get to the part where *you* start talking to *her*?"

I twisted around in my seat. Izzy wasn't exactly fat, but of the four of us who hung out together, she was the roundest. Her face was like a paper plate with two round cheeks colored in with a crayon and a pair of pennies glued on for eyes. Even her hair, which was the same color as her eyes, was a circular frame for all of it.

"Izzy," I said.

"How fast can this car go? The fastest I ever went was 95. My cousin wasn't supposed to be driving that fast, especially with us there. Let's see, there was me, my other cousin—"

"Izzy!"

"What?"

I held up my hand and closed my fingers down over my thumb, like a mouth shutting.

"Yeah, but—"

I did it again, closer to her face. Her cheeks went a darker shade of red crayon.

"You better start talking, Kylie," Jocelyn said to me. "'Cause I'm only giving it about twenty seconds before it gets going again."

"Have you talked to Riannon?" I said.

Izzy's coppery eyes shifted to the right. "Can we stop at a McDonald's?"

"Did you talk to her?" I said.

"Kind of."

"How can you 'kind of' talk to somebody?" I said. And how could you be all chatty-chat-chat one minute and totally forget how to speak the next? Izzy's mouth was in such a tight knot, I was going to have to poke it open with my finger.

"We texted," Izzy said finally. "That's not exactly talking—"

"What did she say?"

"Nothing."

"How can you say nothing in a text?"

"Ky, chill," Jocelyn said out of the side of her mouth. "You're yelling like Mom."

Of course I was yelling. Izzy was making me nuts, just like she always did. Why did I ever think this was a good idea?

"She said she wasn't supposed to talk to you," Izzy said.

"But she gave you a message for me."

"No, she—"

"Yes, she did, Izzy. You just don't know it. What did Mrs. Yeats say to her?"

Some of the terror left Izzy's face. "She didn't tell me *that.*"

"Then what *did* she tell you?"

"That she and Heidi couldn't talk to you—"

"Ohmygosh, Izzy, why are you being so annoying right now?"

"Because she told me not to tell you!"

"Tell me what?"

"That their moms say it's all *your* fault everybody's in trouble. That we all follow you, and if you went off a cliff, we'd go too, and it has to stop!"

I started to sag into my seat belt, but then something caught me. I reached back and crooked a finger into the cuff of Izzy's shorts.

"Their *moms* said that?"

She nodded so hard her hair fell over her eyes.

"O-oh," I said.

Jocelyn was looking in the rearview mirror again. "You probably ought to lay off the kid, Ky. She's practically in tears." She raised her voice. "Hey, Iz, you know there's no crying in Beamers, right?"

"Are you serious?" Izzy said.

"Yeah. It's like a thing."

It really wasn't a thing, but that was okay. I found out what I wanted to know: Heidi's and Riannon's moms really were keeping them from talking to me. At least *they* weren't mad at me. Come to think of it, why had I even considered that? When had they ever been mad at me? We sort of did go over a cliff, but we all held hands and went off together.

Okay, so maybe I had been out in front a little, but that was just the way it always was. Now, I might have to make a plan on my own for a while, until the moms got over it. Besides, I had Izzy to be our messenger. The girl had a gift for that.

"So, Kylie . . . are you going to sit there in a coma, or are you going to come shopping with us?"

I blinked at Jocelyn.

"We're here!" Izzy said. "I am so jazzed. My mom gave me fifty dollars. Do you think that's enough? I want to get flip-flops and a swimsuit and some earrings. What are you getting?"

"Earmuffs," Jocelyn said.

"In the summer?" Izzy said.

I rolled my eyes up as far as they would go. Those moms better get over this fast.

Actually, now that I had a reason to be with Izzy, it was easier to put up with her, especially since Jocelyn was with us. She kept us moving so fast through the stores that I almost didn't have time to get annoyed.

"I have Daddy's American Express card," she said to me as we entered the swimwear section at Macy's. "And I think you should get everything you want."

I usually did get everything I wanted, but that hard look on her face again made me ask why.

"Just because," she said.

"Would this look good on me?"

We both turned to Izzy, who was holding a taxi-cab yellow swimsuit against her that looked like two pieces of yarn with three triangles attached to them.

Before I could blurt out, *Are you serious?* Jocelyn said, "Iz, no. Just no."

The shopping went pretty well after that—how could it not when I ended up with six shopping bags full of new stuff?—except for two things.

One happened when we got to Champs. In one of the windows, they had a display of sports stuff for high schools, and there it was: the most awesome jacket to wear with a cheerleading uniform. "Picture this with your school's logo," the sign said. That wasn't the only thing I could picture. I was already seeing myself shrugging it on only partway, like I didn't care how I looked, and running to join the rest of the squad for the Thursday afternoon game. That was when the seventh grade football team played. That was when I would have been in front of the whole class, all the fans, yelling to my girls, *Ready? Okay!*

"You're drooling, Ky," Jocelyn said, right at my elbow.

"I want that," I said.

"I know." She nudged me with her shoulder. "I said get anything you want, but you should probably wait on this."

I wanted to stomp my foot. Ball up my fists. Call Daddy and tell him to *fix this.*

"You'll get back in," Jocelyn whispered. "And I don't think you'll have to wait long. Money talks."

I said okay and gave the Jacket one last look before we moved on. I wasn't good at waiting for things. I hadn't had that much practice at it.

We had lunch at Carl's Jr., and Izzy's mouth was so busy with a Mile-High burger she only talked about half as much as usual. Although . . . she still managed to make me want to take a bite out of my Styrofoam cup. When Jocelyn said she was going to the restroom, I knew it was because her ears needed a rest.

"I forgot to tell you about this!" Izzy said, spewing mayo across the table.

"Really?" I said and mopped it up with a napkin.

"There's an arts camp starting in Nevada City on Wednesday! At that place that used to be a camp!"

And that deserved an exclamation point?

"Since we didn't get to go to cheerleading camp, we could go to that and still do dance. It's for littler kids, but we could be counselors!"

"*We*?" I asked.

"Yeah. You and me."

I stared at her until she started to pump her straw up and down.

"I'm just sayin'."

I was about to tell her she was a for-real crazy person when her round eyes moved from me to something behind me.

"Uh-oh," she said.

"What?"

I turned my head.

"Don't look!"

"Izzy, *what*?"

"Victoria-My-Pet alert."

That was our nickname for Tori Taylor.

"Just her?"

"No. The Drama Queen is with her. Of course. They're like attached with duct tape or something—"

"What are they doing?"

"Going into Claire's. Naturally. They sell cheap jewelry in there. Little *girl* jewelry . . ."

I let Izzy keep on talking because I wasn't listening to her anyway. I was trying to decide whether to turn around. Why would I want to see Tori Taylor if I didn't have to? She had everything that used to be mine, and looking at her only reminded me of that.

So why did I swivel in my seat in slow motion, while Izzy droned on and on like the teacher in the Peanuts movies?

Maybe it was so I could see her with one puny bag from Claire's when I had six from high-end stores she couldn't even think about going into.

Or maybe I was hoping she actually *had* gotten pimples since I left school. Or she was getting fat. Anything that would make people not want to follow her and her stupid Code.

Or just maybe I wanted her to see *me* with my cool big sister and Izzy so she'd know I wasn't all by myself and heartbroken like she thought I was. Like she probably hoped I was.

Whatever the reason, when I finally got all the way twisted around, she came out of Claire's with *no* shopping bags. And no acne. And she was taller and skinnier than I remembered her, with her chocolate-brown hair cut shorter so she looked older too.

She didn't even glance in my direction. She was too busy nodding at that huge-eyed Ophelia like she was Taylor Swift or somebody to even notice there was anyone else in the entire mall. Then Ophelia waved one of her arms out the way she was always doing because she thought she was this actress, and Tori laughed. A laugh I could see all over her face. Her happy face.

Ophelia flung the arm around Tori's shoulder, and they tripped over themselves catching up with Tori's mom. She laughed, too, until they were swallowed up in the crowd and I couldn't see them laughing anymore.

I thought Izzy said, "She thinks she's all that now," but another tinier voice was somehow louder.

I don't have that. I've never had that.

"There are still stores we haven't hit," Jocelyn said.

I didn't even know she'd come back from the restroom.

"I'm done," I said "Let's go home."

Chapter Four

I am not a morning person, especially in the summer, but the next day I got up even grumpier than usual. Whenever that happened, my dad would look at Mom and say, "Is it time for her to start drinking coffee yet?"

That day, Monday, he stopped on his way through the kitchen door to the garage, wearing a smooth lavender shirt and the tie I gave him for his birthday, and made that wiggly line with his eyebrows.

"Do we need some attitude adjustment this morning, princess?"

Mom grunted over the huge mug she was cradling in her hands. "She doesn't look much like a princess right now. Kylie, could you scowl just a little harder?"

"That Lydia person is coming today, right?" I said.

"She is," Dad said, "and she's your ticket to getting that A."

"She hates me," I said.

The eyebrows crinkled. "Who could hate you?"

Everybody.

"You need this grade, so let's go for it. Okay? Are we good?"

We weren't, so I didn't answer. But when he was gone, I turned to my mom, who was refilling the giant mug.

"You're going to be around while she's here, right?"

"What?"

"When Lydia's here? You said you'd be around."

"Yes, I'll be around. Now go back to bed. She's not coming until one, and you're cranky."

Cranky wasn't even the word. Try *ready to pinch off somebody's head.*

By the time Lydia arrived that afternoon, my pink T-shirt and shorts were covered in so much cat hair that I looked like I was growing black fur. I'd spent most of the morning hugging Margaret and telling her that I wished I had her life. Except that she couldn't do a cartwheel.

Mom obviously didn't notice my hairy condition as she led Lydia into the library where we were going to do "the thing," as Mom put it. I didn't know any people who had a library in their house, and nobody in *our* house really used it. There definitely wasn't anything in there I wanted to read.

Lydia looked pretty impressed with it. Of course, she had to stand on tiptoes to see higher than the first shelves.

"I see you drove here," Mom said, standing in the doorway with her arms folded across the top she wore to play tennis. The sparkly bracelet Dad gave her for her birthday looked even sparklier dangling from her tanned wrist.

Lydia looked like Mom had said something funny. "I did."

"How is that possible? I'm sorry—" Although Mom didn't look like she was sorry at all. "I'm just curious about how you're able to drive."

"I have special controls," Lydia said. "Basically, I can do everything anyone else does."

Except see the top shelves. I kept my mouth shut, mostly because Mom was doing a great job without my help.

"Amazing," Mom said. "So you don't need anything in here? Phone book to sit on?"

Lydia actually laughed. "I brought my own little booster seat. I'm fine."

"You certainly handle it better than I would. All right then, you'll be done in an hour and a half—is that correct?"

"Yes," Lydia said.

Mom poked at her phone, probably setting the timer. She did that for everything, including when she was on it with somebody she didn't want to talk to. It would ding, and she'd say, "I'm *sorry*, I have to hang up. I have an appointment."

Done with that, Mom said, "If you need to use the restroom, there's a powder room across the hall. The housekeeper uses that one, but she isn't here today, so it's all yours."

Lydia just nodded, and I wondered how she could even move her head. It was bigger than most people's, and then there was all that dark curly hair. I bet my mom was thinking about what the right stylist could do for her. Or not. She was actually acting like Lydia wasn't all that important. She was mostly like that with everybody.

By then Lydia was positioning a little red seat that looked like a kid's booster in a restaurant onto one of the leather chairs at the library table. I sat down while she climbed up and settled on it as if she were a queen on a throne. Which she so was not.

"Let's start with a question," I said.

Lydia closed the folder she had started to open. "All right."

"How long is this going to take?"

Lydia gave me a look with nothing in it. "Ninety minutes. Did you miss that part?"

She smiled then, but I ignored it.

"Sorry," I said. "I meant, like, how many days."

"I think we're measuring more in weeks." The folder came open.

"Oh," I said. "I guess they didn't tell you that I'm a straight-A student."

Lydia tapped the folder. "Actually *they* did. Your grades are very impressive."

"So . . . it isn't going to take me weeks to do a social studies project. Tell me what I'm supposed to do, and I'll have it done in, like, a weekend."

"I see." Lydia folded her hands into a little stack of short fingers. "Anything else?"

There *was*, but I didn't want to ask because it was going to sound like I didn't know something I should know, and I hated that. But I was also kind of desperate.

"Are you doing this with Heidi and Riannon too?" I tilted my head so my hair covered one eye. "I would ask them, but their moms are being . . . they're incommunicado."

I hoped that was the right word. Apparently, it was because Lydia didn't have the "Isn't that precious?" look grown-ups got on their faces when you used a big word and messed it up.

"I am not working with Heidi and Riannon," she said. "I assume you have a reason for asking."

I did, but right then I couldn't remember what it was. My insides were steaming. Why was I the only one who had to go through this? Heidi and Riannon had done everything I'd done and in some cases more. Why weren't they sitting here too?

"Never mind," I said between my teeth.

"I'm sorry, I didn't hear you."

"I said never *mind*."

She looked at me for what seemed like forever, until I was about to go *What?* and then she finally said, "Back to your question about how long this is going to take."

Yeah, let's get back to that.

"I'm sure you could do a fabulous research project in a week. You're obviously bright. Creative." She swept her gaze around the library. "You have all the resources."

It was my turn to stare *her* down. I was having to practically eat the inside of my cheek to keep back, *So what's the problem?*

"The problem is . . ."

I felt my eyes bug out like Jocelyn's did. Had I actually said it, or did being a dwarf mean she could read people's minds?

"The problem is," she said again, "you've used your gifts for the wrong things. It takes a smart girl with a lot of imagination to pull off the kind of bullying you and your friends did and come very close to getting away with it."

I gritted my teeth harder. How much did I hate that word *bullying*? It made it sound like we were criminals.

Lydia kept going. "So, yes, you're required to do a project for Mr. Jett so you can pass social studies."

"Just so you know," I said. "I can't just pass. I have to get an A. I *always* get an A."

"Duly noted," Lydia said. "But that isn't what this is really about. Our work together is going to be about how you treat people, and your project will be related to that."

I could barely stay in the seat at that point. "So what's the assignment?"

"That's what we're going to figure out. Over time."

"How *much* time?"

"As much time as it takes. I hope by the end of July."

"That's practically the whole summer!"

Lydia didn't say anything. If she didn't stop just sitting there looking at me all calm and tidy and folded, I was going to scream. Just scream. Because I didn't know what else to do.

"This clearly wasn't what you expected," Lydia said. "I explained it to your mom and dad."

"I didn't get the memo," I said.

Her throat made a rustling sound. Oh. She was laughing.

"What's funny?" I said.

"I enjoy your dry sense of humor," she said. "Another one of your gifts that could be put to good use."

Whatever. All I knew was this wasn't going to take until the end *July*. Cheerleading practice started right about then. I had to be reinstituted or reinstalled or whatever "re" it was before that.

"We should get started then," I said.

Lydia nodded the hair and reached into a red bag so big she could have curled up in it like Margaret. I expected the social studies book, but she pulled out a pad of paper and a pink gel pen and slid it across the table to me.

"I want you to make a list," she said, "of all the mean things you said and did to Ginger from the time she started at your school."

"Are you serious?" I said.

"As a compound fracture," she said. "Let me know when you're finished."

She hopped down from the chair and went over to the cases where Dad had a bunch of lawyer books lined up. I stared down at the pad. It looked kind of like how my mind felt. A complete blank.

Mean Things I Did to Ginger, I wrote across the top.

I dragged the pen across the paper without making a mark so Lydia would think I was writing. But I couldn't put down anything.

In the first place, define *mean*. For people to be mean to me, which they never were, they'd have to steal my boyfriend, which they never could, or take away cheerleading. So basically, I knew some mean people, but they weren't me.

Was I supposed to write down what *Ginger* considered mean? How could I know that? It seemed like everything was mean in her opinion. She tried to be in our group, and we told her, like, a thousand times we didn't need anybody else, and she kept pushing. When we finally said, *Go away!* she got all hurt, and Tori and *her* friends decided we were the mean girls.

"How's it going?" Lydia said. She was climbing back into her seat.

"I hope this isn't part of my grade," I said, "because I can't think of anything."

Lydia made a little "huh" sound. "That's interesting because I don't think Ginger would have any trouble at all filling up that entire pad. In a way, she did."

She fished around in the bag again and brought out a small spiral notebook, which I thought was brand new until she opened it and flipped through the pages. Almost every one was filled with writing. It looked a little bit familiar.

"Ginger gave me permission to share some of this with you," Lydia said.

"She wrote all that?"

"She did."

I wanted to ask what it was, but I didn't want to seem that interested. Still . . .

"If it's about all the supposedly mean things we did to her, no offense because I know you like her and everything, but that's just her opinion."

Lydia looked at the first page.

Was I talking to myself here?

"Things I Decided Not to Say," she read.

"I don't get it," I said.

"Instead of blurting out whatever burst into her head, Ginger wrote those things down first so she could decide what she actually did want coming out of her mouth."

Oh, yeah. I remembered that now. But this had what to do me?

"Since most of this was in response to you, she wrote down what you said first. It's kind of like a movie script. I'll read you some."

It wasn't going to do me any good to protest, but I didn't actually have to listen. I had a whole skill set for making teachers think I was paying attention when I was thinking about something more important.

Lydia read:

Kylie: Heidi says that woman's (Lydia's) class is fascinating. I wish you didn't have to act mean to be in there.

What I didn't say: If that was true, you could practically teach the class.

"Do you remember that, Kylie?" Lydia said.

"No," I said. Maybe I did, but this was so none of her business.

Lydia read some more.

Kylie: I shouldn't have to lock all my things up.

What I didn't say: You mean all your nice things you think everybody wants?

"How about that one?" she said.

"I don't see what was mean about that."

"If I'm not mistaken, you were setting things up so you could accuse Tori of stealing your poem. Ring any bells now?"

Maybe she'd stop if I admitted it, so I said, "I guess."

Lydia looked back at the notebook.

Kylie: (talking about Mr. Devon under her breath) What a freak.

What I didn't do: Pop her one.

"I didn't say that," I said. "Riannon did."

My voice sounded whiney. What was going on here? I wasn't a whiner. I was the one who made *other* people whine.

Lydia closed the notebook, and I stole a look at the clock that hung between two of the bookcases. We had used up exactly fifteen minutes. It might be time to run screaming from the room.

The only thing that stopped me was Lydia saying, "Let's try something different." She nodded at the pad. "New page. I want you to list your rivals."

"You mean like enemies?" There might not be enough sheets of paper in that pad.

"Other kids who threaten to take you down."

I didn't wait for her to give me further instructions, and I had the list done in about two minutes:

Tori Taylor

Ophelia Smith

Winnie George

Michelle Iann

Ginger Hollingberry

Shelby Ryan

I finished with, *And everybody who says they believe in the Code.*

"Done," I said and put down the pink gel pen.

"May I have it?" Lydia said.

I handed it to her, glad I didn't put her name on there. I'm not a moron.

But she didn't even look at it. She held it up, tore it in half, and ripped those halves in half and again until my list was practically confetti on the table.

"Do you know why I did that?" she said.

"Uh, no."

"Because there *are* no rivals, my dear. None of your peers has any more power than anybody else. The only power any of you have is the power to be who you were made to be, and every one of you has it in equal amounts."

She reached into the bag again, the one that was making me think of Mary Poppins, and came out this time with a card. I almost groaned out loud. I'd seen ones like it before when Tori and the G.G.s showed them to us in their science presentation about people being mean. They were always pulling them out of their pockets, especially Ginger, like they were reading instructions on what to do next. Can you say, "lame"?

"This your first personal Code Card," Lydia said, pushing it toward me.

I didn't pick it up, but I couldn't help looking at it. Big green letters said, There Are No Rivals.

"This is to remind you," Lydia said.

"I'm not being mean when I say this . . ." It was like I was measuring out my words in spoons. "But I don't want this."

"You don't have to want it, but you do need it."

"I don't *need* anything that Tori Taylor made up! It's like *she's* punishing me!"

So much for the measuring spoons.

Lydia shook her head. "Nobody's punishing you."

"Mrs. Yeats is."

"You're receiving the consequences of your actions from Mrs. Yeats. As for me . . ." Lydia pressed both hands to her chest. "I'm here because what you've done is bad, but you yourself are not."

No . . . I'm not.

Lydia leaned into the table to look at me. If she had heard the wee voice, I really was going to run screaming from the room.

"You can't argue with that one, can you?" she said. "You're not a bad person."

"That's what I keep trying to tell everybody," I said.

"Using all the wrong voices."

I dug my fingernails into the chair pad.

"This is about getting you healed."

"From what?"

"The need to be mean."

"I'm never mean to anybody without a reason!"

"There is never a reason to be mean. And that's where we're going to start."

What just happened? How did she get me digging a hole in the chair and saying stuff I didn't want to say? The next thing you knew, she'd be making me cry, and just so you know, I never cried, not for real. Not since Margaret left.

So I took in a deep breath and folded *my* hands on the table so that my sparkle-pink nails were all in a row.

"Tell me what I have to do, and I'll do it."

Half of Lydia's mouth smiled. "Our work together isn't going to be about jumping through hoops so you can be reinstated at school and be a cheerleader again and go back to the way you were."

She was reading my mind anyway, so I went ahead and said, "See, I don't get what was wrong with the way I was. That was all fine until Ginger . . . and then Tori—"

"Kylie."

"What?"

"Look at all you've lost because of your behavior. Do you think the same behavior is going to get that back?"

I closed my eyes. Maybe that would make her stop.

"Enough of that for now." Lydia leaned back in the chair and parked her folded hands under her chin like a little shelf. "What do you like to do?"

I was surprised because I answered right away. "I like cheerleading and all the stuff that goes with it. Dance. Gymnastics."

"Can you talk more about that?"

Whoa. Wait just a minute. Now she was trying to get on my good side. Not happening.

I shrugged. "There isn't anything else to say about it. I just like it."

She nodded like I'd actually told her something, which I had *not*. "I think we're good for today," she said finally. "Homework assignment for Thursday. Make a list of everything you do to stay popular."

"We're done?" I said.

"We are."

At least the assignment is stupid-easy, I thought after I closed the front door behind her. I didn't have to *do* anything to stay popular. I just was.

Wasn't I?

Chapter Five

After Lydia left, my first stop was the kitchen where Mom was sitting at the snack bar with her laptop and a glass of that diet stuff she drank. She was always on a diet.

"I'm looking at furniture for your room," she said, without looking at *me*.

"I thought you were going to be around while she was here," I said.

"I didn't go anywhere." Mom glanced down at the bottom of her computer screen. "Good. You're done early. I can do some practice shots before the match."

"You have to find somebody else to tutor me."

She kept her eyes on me as she drained the glass. "You're going to have to deal with it. It's the only way you're passing social studies."

"But we're not even talking about social studies—"

"Kylie—seriously—you're getting on my last nerve. Just do it, all right? Sometimes you have to just do it." She handed me the glass. "Put this in the dishwasher for me, will you?"

I waited until she went out the door to the garage, and then I put the glass on the counter and stomped up to the suite. Jocelyn came out of the closet dressed to go someplace.

"Sheesh, I thought it was the Clydesdales coming through here."

I threw myself on the bed.

"I see your session went well."

"I'm not doing this." The only reason I didn't pick up a pillow and hurl it across the room was because Margaret appeared and tapped my face with her whipped cream paw.

"That bad, huh?"

"She wants to heal me."

"I didn't know you were sick."

"I'm not, but *she* thinks I am, and if I don't 'get healed,' I don't get to go back to school."

Jocelyn slipped on a filmy sweater thing over her white tank. "So get healed."

"Huh?"

"Just fake it. That's what I do when the only way out is to give them what they want. Just fake it till you make it. I do it with Dad all the time."

"Are you serious?"

"It's the only way I've stayed sane around here. That and my car and my friends." Jocelyn slung a silver purse the size of a party invitation over her shoulder by its long strap and headed for the door. "You can totally do this, Ky."

When she was gone, I let my head fall back into the pile of pillows. Jocelyn had so many of them that it took forever just to get in bed at night. Margaret took her place in the middle of my chest and nudged my chin with her head. That meant: *Where were you?*

"In the library," I said in an almost-wee voice. "I know, weird, right? I would have taken you with me, but Mom doesn't want cat hair on the rug in the room nobody goes into." I scratched between her ears. "It doesn't make sense to me either."

She blinked her yellow eyes at me. *What did you do? Who did you see?*

"The shortest person ever. With the most hair. We did silly stuff. I didn't like it."

Margaret's ears perked up in two perfect pink triangles. *Did she like you?*

"She said I wasn't a bad person."

Ah.

The eyes closed, and Margaret purred herself to sleep. Something started happening to me, something in my throat. It took me a minute to remember that it was the Missing Margaret feeling. Nanny Margaret.

It took me *less* than a minute to roll Kitty Margaret into the pillows and get up. I didn't hang out with that feeling. Not ever.

I'm lonely.

Not happening.

I looked around for the remote, and my eyes fell on Jocelyn's computer. What was I even thinking? This was the perfect time to check my e-mail. The Minnie Moms must have given up by now, right?

Apparently not because the only e-mail I had was from Izzy, who I wasn't in the mood for, so I almost didn't open it. But the subject line said You Have to Know About This. Which could have meant she got new toothpaste. But it could also mean she'd done her dachshund thing and gotten me some information about Ri and Heidi.

I clicked it open. At least there was only one sentence from Izzy: *Read this, but don't freak out.*

The rest of it was a forward from Riannon and Heidi, using the account we had together called K4Fair—Kylie for Fairness—back when we first started to fight the Code thing. It looked like it was long, so I crossed my legs in the chair and got comfy.

If you want to know what really happened, read this, they'd written.

Of *course* I wanted to know what happened. What did they think I'd been waiting for the last five days?

After you read it, scroll to the bottom to see what to do next.

Oh, so now they were telling *me* what to do? Whatever, Heidi and Ri. I read on.

The Chin Freak is evil. She's making me do hours of working in the slums with homeless people. Ha! Like she could really make me do that! Like my dad would even let me! You are the ones who are going to end up doing it. Just wait.

I read that over again. Why did it sound like I wrote it, only way . . . uglier? What were they even talking about? When it didn't make sense to me the second time I read it, I kept going.

You didn't pass Mr. Traitor Jett's class, did you? Because if I did, you shouldn't. You should have to work with crazy Dwarf Lady too. I shouldn't have to take all the punishment when I didn't do half of what you did. Just because I made you do it doesn't matter. You still did it.

I blinked hard and fast as I continued—

This is all about that stupid Code thing, and now they're going to make me follow it or I don't get to do anything. I can't believe this is happening, but I'll find a way to stop it, and it won't be pretty. You are never coming here for a sleepover again. This is my plan now, and you are out.

Signed,

Kylie Steppe

It hit me straight in the face. They had taken the e-mail I wrote them and twisted it. But why? Why would they do that and send it to me? Did they lose their minds while they were on Internet lockdown?

There was more, and I had to read it or I was never going to know what was going on.

The next part of the e-mail was separated from the rest by a row of stars. Below that, they'd written:

Now you see what she's really like and how she bullied us too. It's totally her fault that we got expelled. We can't let her get away with it, and we need your help. Spread the word that she is poison by following this account on Instagram: @K4Fair. #TrueK

Who were they talking to? Who were they asking to help them?

I looked up at the top of the e-mail, and for the first time, I saw a whole long paragraph of names. I lost count after forty.

My fingers shook as I grabbed the mouse and closed the e-mail so I wouldn't have to look at it anymore. What I did need to look at was Instagram. What kind of pictures were they posting on there?

I dragged my hands through my hair. Ohmygoshohmygoshohmy-gosh. They were saying stuff about me. Stuff that wasn't even true. How was I supposed to find out what it was when I didn't have a phone or an iPad or anyplace to see it? Could I open it on this computer? I didn't know how, but I was smart, right? I could figure it out—

"Kylie."

I almost fell out of the chair. Mom. Opening the door. I dropped to the floor and did three forward rolls toward her.

"What are you doing?" she said.

"Practicing."

"You better not have been on that computer."

I sat up. "What are you doing back so soon?"

Mom frowned, pinching in that place between her eyebrows over her nose. "Nobody showed up. It's too hot for tennis, anyway. I'm going out to the pool. You should too. You're spending too much time holed up in here."

"I'll be out in a minute," I said.

She was saying "No computer" again as she faded down the stairs. I looked hopelessly at Jocelyn's laptop. If I was going to find out exactly what was happening, I was going to have to depend on Izzy. I didn't have any choice.

And I wasn't used to not having any choice.

I sank to the edge of the bed, and Margaret joined me, although I only half-noticed her.

There had to be a choice. I never just sat around and waited for stuff to happen to me. I made it happen, didn't I? Wasn't I the one who did that?

I sucked in air that tasted like Jocelyn's body spray. Okay, here it was: Heidi and Riannon were only doing this because they had to do whatever it took to get back in school and on the squad. They had to make it look like everything was all my fault and they were innocent. Fine. I would do whatever it took too. With them or without them.

But I can't do it by myself.

"Shut *up*!" I said. And this time, I did throw a pillow across the room.

Margaret scurried under the bed.

∾

When I got up the next morning—okay, afternoon—Mom was sitting in the breakfast nook talking on her phone. Big surprise. I padded into the kitchen barefoot, so I guess she didn't hear me at first.

"You totally could've called," she said in a voice that made me glad she wasn't pointing those words at *me*. It also made me back up around the corner to listen.

"I still don't get what you're doing . . . It's just stupid. . . . That has nothing to do with us . . . Oh, come on, get real. Girls have always done this . . . *I* did it . . . I'm sorry, what? . . . Did you actually just say that to me? Well, let me say this to you . . ."

I heard Mom's hand slap the table, which made me jump and knock my elbow against the wall. There was a funky pause. I knew she'd heard me.

"I can't talk about this right now," she said, "but we so will because I'm not done with you. . . . Fine, then. If that's the way you want to play it. Don't need it. Or you."

I stepped around the corner, yawning and stretching like I'd sleepwalked all the way down the stairs. Even then it took Mom a second to look up at me. She was staring at the phone she'd let fall to the table. She looked . . . confused, and that wasn't an expression I saw on her face very often.

"Do we have any waffles?" I said.

She shook her head like she wanted to move stuff around inside it and pointed to the freezer. "You're doing a day/night reversal, Kylie."

"Huh?"

"Staying up all night and sleeping all day."

"It's summer."

"Well, that's going to cease and desist tomorrow."

I pulled my head out of the freezer, Eggos in hand. "Why?"

"Mrs. Yeats called."

"She changed her mind?"

"No, she did not change her mind. That would take an act of Congress."

Mom went to the pantry and came out with a bottle of pancake syrup. The sugar-free kind, which was nasty.

"She said she has a community service project for you, and

since I haven't had time to come up with anything, we're going with it."

I lost my appetite for waffles. "What is it?"

"It's assisting a teacher at an arts camp for underprivileged kids in Nevada City. They need help with the dance program." Mom pushed the toaster toward me. "And you know every one of those little girls thinks she wants to be a cheerleader."

I lost my appetite for *everything*.

"You wanted to go to cheerleading camp," she said.

"This isn't *real* cheerleading camp. This is like a wannabe thing."

Mom plunked a spray bottle of I Can't Believe It's Not Butter next to the syrup and tossed back her hair. "Do you have another plan right now? We're not getting around this community service thing. It's happening, and it's happening tomorrow morning at eight o'clock."

"Mo-om!"

"We're done, Kylie." She tapped the toaster with her white-tipped fingernail. "This waffle isn't going to cook unless you push down the lever."

I dove for the table where her phone was. "I'm calling Dad."

"You don't have to call him. He's here."

"Where?"

"Out by the pool. He's talking to the guy—"

I left her phone spinning on the table top and yanked open the door that led onto the back deck. Dad was below, facing the house and talking to somebody I couldn't see.

"Dad!" I said.

He looked up and shielded his eyes with his hand. "Hey, princess."

"I have to talk to you!"

I didn't wait for him to answer. I just took the steps two at a time and vaulted over the railing on the last landing, already wailing, "I'm not doing all this stuff Mrs. Yeats said. I'm not!"

Dad's eyebrows pulled together in the middle, and I knew I should stop right there, but I couldn't.

"You have to make her let me back in. I can't do all this stupid stuff!"

"Not a good time, Kylie." Dad's eyes shifted to whomever he was talking to and back to me. "We'll talk later."

"We need to talk *now*. It's getting worse and you have to—"

"I said later. I'm tied up at the moment."

Just like always, he was all into somebody more important than me. Like who?

I looked at the person he now turned back to: the big redheaded guy with a tool belt around his waist and freckles on his lips. *He* was more important than *me*? *Ginger's father?*

"Seriously?" I said. "Really?"

Dad cupped his hand under my elbow and at the same time looked at Mr. Hollingberry. "Wait here. I need to take care of this."

I was still too angry to feel triumphant, but at least he was going to listen to me. Or so I thought, until we were all the way inside the pool house and the door was closed behind us. It was dark except for the rectangle of sunlight that streamed in from the up-high window. Dad let go of me and stabbed his hands onto his hips. Even in the dimness, I could see that his eyebrows were so tangled up they might never come apart.

"Kylie," he said in a very low voice.

The lower my dad's voice got, the madder he was. I could hardly hear it.

"Do not *ever* interrupt me when I'm doing business. Are we clear?"

"I didn't know that was business. It's just the construction guy."

"And you made both of us look like idiots in front of him. Is that the impression you want to give the people who work for me? Because it's not the one *I'm* going for."

"Mrs. *Yeats* wants to make me look like an idiot."

"What?"

"This stupid camp thing—"

"That's what this is about?"

"Yes!"

Dad pinched the top of his nose between two fingers. I didn't recognize *that* signal, but it didn't look like a good one. Still—steam was building up inside my face.

"You know, I hate to admit this," Dad said, "but she could have a point."

"Mrs. *Yeats?*"

"It's not a bad idea for you to learn some self-control in certain situations."

I was already shaking my head. No. Nonononononono.

"Do the camp, princess. It'll do you good, even for getting into Roseville."

He tapped my nose. I pulled away.

"Fine. Do it the hard way." He put his forehead close to mine. "But you're going to do it."

I waited until he was out of the pool house before I let the steam blow out of my ears. At least that's the way it felt. But it didn't help, not if I had to go to that stupid camp anyway. And deal with little kids from bad neighborhoods who didn't know anything about dance or gymnastics and were . . . different . . . way different from me.

"It's going to be horrible," I said out loud even though Margaret wasn't there.

It's going to be scary.

I'm not scared!

Because I don't know how to be around people who are different from me.

I pushed a blue-and-white-striped cushion from the bench to the floor and stomped on it.

It didn't make me feel any better.

Chapter Six

I might as well just say it right out: I hated that camp from the minute I stepped onto the property at what used to be a summer place for rich kids back in the olden days. It was up at the top of a hill with all these pine trees towering over it like guards saying, *You will participate or else.* I didn't even have to see the "dance studio" (whatever *that* was going to look like) or the "Gathering Place" that the sign pointed to. Mom tried to show it to me on the Internet the night before, but I refused to look at it.

I didn't need any of that to make me hate it. All it took was for Izzy and me—yeah, I made her go with me—to see the rest of the "assistant teachers" standing in front of a table at the top of the outside amphitheater thing, the Gathering Place.

There they were—

Tori Taylor. Ginger Hollingberry. Ophelia Smith. Michelle Iann. Winnie George. Shelby Ryan.

It was like before Lydia tore up my Rivals list somebody photocopied it and invited everybody who was on it. This had Mrs. Yeats' fingerprints all over it. Or maybe Lydia's.

"That's not good," Izzy whispered to me.

"They're getting name badges," I said. "Go get ours."

Izzy headed for the table, squeezing between two knots of girls way younger than us. I was making a mental survey of them—Walmart clothes, Payless shoes, Cost Cutters haircuts—when someone behind me said, "Kylie! I'm glad you decided to come."

I was about to tell whomever it was that I did not "decide" to come, but when I turned around it was Mrs. Bernstein who was smiling into my face. I didn't recognize her voice at first because she didn't call me "Señorita Kylie" like she did when she was teaching our Spanish class. She was a cool teacher with a black ponytail and a funny sense of humor and pretty eyebrows, and she was an even cooler cheerleading coach.

Until she dumped me.

"You and Izzy are going to be my assistants," she said. "We have six little first and second graders. I think it's going to be a blast."

I didn't see how Mrs. Bernstein could possibly believe that. She used to be a San Francisco Forty-Niners cheerleader. This was like—like wearing a prom dress to go to McDonald's. She could at least be teaching at the *real* cheerleading camp.

Izzy came back then and handed me a plastic badge that said KYLIE! in big orange letters and in smaller ones, "Assistant Dance Coach." It was attached to an orange-and-brown lanyard to be hung around my neck. It didn't match my pink-and-purple-striped tank top at all.

"They'll have T-shirts for you by next week," Mrs. Bernstein said as she tightened her ponytail. "They wanted to make sure they had everybody's sizes right."

I looked at hers, which was brown with orange letters. Until now I had never seen her wear anything that wasn't totally on trend. I didn't make that up. My mom said it about her after every parent-teacher conference.

Vowing that I was going to get a different lanyard before tomorrow, I hung it around my neck and watched the chattering flock of kids go down the wooden steps like ducklings and file into the benches made from cut-in-half logs. Tori and her followers were right behind them, all talky and excited like this was a huge deal.

Actually, Michelle—whom everybody called Mitch—didn't look that excited because she never did. She was square-shaped and had short, poky hair, and she acted tough. Okay, so she *was* tough. As she turned her head in my direction, I sucked in air. But when she saw me, she pulled up her chin and then nodded like she was saying, *What's up?*

What's *up?* What was up was that all the G.G.s were there acting like this whole thing was *their* idea, and here I was with Izzy and had *no* idea what this was about. I didn't need the wee voice to tell me I was freaking out. I needed information.

As Mrs. Bernstein nudged Izzy and me down the steps of the amphitheater, I asked, "Are all the assistants working with the dance team?"

"No." She nodded us into a log seat row and sat between Izzy and me. "Ophelia and Ginger are working with the drama group, Shelby and Winnie are helping the writing group, and Mitch and Tori, now theirs is a little different. It's called the production group. Not sure what that's about."

I didn't really care what that was about. She could have stopped at no. At least I didn't have to work with them.

The chatter started to die down because a guy with a gray ponytail and wearing wrinkled pants and Birkenstocks came to the front.

"That's the librarian," Izzy whispered to me.

"I *know*," I said.

I wasn't really irritated with her. I was annoyed because the guy, Mr. Devon, was yet another person from our school who thought Ginger was like a child genius or something.

"Good morning, fellow artists," he said. "I'm Mr. Devon, and I will be leading our journey of the imagination this summer."

I couldn't help it. I had to roll my eyes. These kids were going to eat him for lunch if he kept talking to them like he was Shakespeare.

"Bravo!" someone called out. It sounded like Ophelia. Who else?

The entire crowd gave a giggle in unison, but Ophelia stood and said, "Come on, fellow artists. Bravo for Sir Devon!"

They yelled that about fifty times, and then Mr. Devon got them back under control. It was more of the same stuff for the next fifteen minutes. He could have just told us in plain *English* that we would meet first thing every morning here in the Gathering Place and then we'd work in our groups and come back together in the "dining hall" (which I was pretty sure was just a cafeteria) for lunch. I didn't see why we couldn't just go home for lunch because the camp day was finished at eleven thirty. He said sometimes we would meet again before lunch to share what we were doing, especially as we got closer to the Grand Finale.

We couldn't get there fast enough as far as I was concerned.

By the time Mrs. Bernstein, Izzy, and I led our six "dancers" along the pine-needle path to the building we were using for a studio, they were all saying things like "alas" and "forsooth," even though they didn't know what any of it meant. I didn't either.

"Ladies," Mrs. Bernstein said, "let's take our shoes off out here and carry them in so we don't damage our dance floor."

Oh please.

But I was surprised when we walked—well, I walked; they all

ran—into a soft-white room with full-length mirrors on one wall and a spongy black floor like they had in the studio I used to go to. I counted as the girls lined up their shoes against another wall and hung their backpacks on pegs. There really were only six of them, but it seemed like there had to be more. They were making enough racket for six*teen*.

Mrs. Bernstein sat them in a wiggly half circle in the middle of the room with their backs to the mirror. That was smart because not one of them could take her eyes off her own reflection for seven seconds.

"Tell us your names, please, ladies," Mrs. Bernstein said.

They did.

There was Callie, with legs that looked like they came straight out of her neck—they were that long. Felicity, whose belly showed between the bottom of her *Frozen* T-shirt and the top of a skirt with an elastic waistband. Daniella, of the Wet Lips and Wet Eyes. And Pilar, the one who had black hair down to her waist and could barely speak English. I hoped there wasn't going to be a test because by the time we got to the last two, I couldn't remember any of their names, and they were always playing with their name tags, so who could read them?

"And what's your name, Milady?" Mrs. Bernstein said to the curly-haired blonde who, if I had to pick, was the pretty one in the room.

"Why are you calling us 'milady'?" she asked.

"Because it's fun, for one thing," Mrs. Bernstein said.

"I don't think it's fun. I think it's dumb."

I kind of had to agree with her there.

"Then what shall I call you?" Mrs. Bernstein asked.

"My name."

"Which is?"

Curls held up her name tag.

Mrs. Bernstein nodded. "Abigail. Do you prefer that or Abby?"

The kid let her bottom lip drop open. "It *says* Abigail."

"Then Abigail it is."

I stared at Mrs. Bernstein as she turned to the last girl. I couldn't believe she didn't kick that little brat right out of the class. Talk about rude. No way I was calling her Abigail. Her name was Attitude.

"May I call *you* Milady?" Mrs. Bernstein said to the final girl.

She had the sandy kind of blonde hair that somebody had tried to curl and didn't know what she was doing, so it was all dented and stuck out in weird places. Her brown eyes practically took up the whole top half of her face.

"My name's Nichole," she said and glanced at Attitude. "Not Nicky."

"I'll make a note of it," Mrs. Bernstein said.

"Why do you have to do that?" Attitude asked. "It's right there on her name tag."

Mrs. Bernstein ignored her that time and asked the "ladies" to line up, again facing away from the mirror, so she could find out what they already knew.

"I've been taking dance since I was two," Attitude informed her.

Who could tell? The whole time Mrs. Bernstein was having them do leaps and pliés, Attitude did her own thing. Or yawned. Or gazed at herself from every angle.

And everything Attitude did . . . Nichole copied her. I decided to call her Xerox.

Izzy and I stood at the front on opposite sides of Mrs. Bernstein and demonstrated what she did, which was way easy. None of the little girls except Attitude and Xerox seemed to think so. Felicity, the one with too much midriff showing under the faded-out *Frozen* T-shirt, latched her eyes onto me and tried so hard to do what I was doing that her whole head turned red. She couldn't do any of it. But at the end, when Mrs. Bernstein told them all they'd done fabulously well—was she even *there?*—Felicity bounced up and down and pumped her fist in the air and yelled, "Bravo!"

Three hours down. One hundred seventeen left to go.

I might die.

I thought that was bad, but I hadn't been to lunch yet.

For the time we were in the studio, I didn't have to think about who else was there, but it hit me in the face again when Izzy and I went to the "dining hall." It actually was like something out of *Harry Potter*, with dark wood walls and round tables with big baskets of fruit in the middle of them. While the kids and the rest of the assistants were doing the *oo-ah* thing and running for tables, I had a sinking-down feeling I'd never had before, ever.

I didn't know where my table was.

Even on the first day at Gold Country Middle School last September, I knew right where my posse was supposed to sit: in the middle, of course, where we could see everybody. I even knew which chair was mine, also in the middle, and so did Riannon and Heidi and Izzy and Shelby.

Everyone else in sixth grade knew which table was ours too, and no one ever tried to sit there without an invitation.

Except Ginger.

"Where are we sitting?" Izzy asked.

I looked for Mrs. Bernstein, but it was obvious all the adult teachers were eating together. Going over there would be like barging into the faculty lounge.

The little kids had already rushed to fill up their tables, where they were having sword fights with the bananas and trying to juggle the apples. The only other table was the one with a flag sticking out of the fruit basket where someone had written "Awesome Teaching Assistants!" Tori and the rest of them were settling themselves into chairs, and there were two seats left.

Izzy started to say, "Are we—"

"Are you serious?"

"Then where do we—"

"I'm calling my mom," I said. "She's taking me to Burger King or something."

"You got your cell phone back?"

"No!"

"Then how are you going to call her?"

"Izzy, will you just hush up and let me think?"

Izzy did, but it didn't do any good. All I could do was watch Shelby share an apple with Ginger like they were doing a scene from *Snow White*. Winnie whispered something in Mitch's ear, and Ophelia said something that made the whole table laugh. Just as I was about to turn away, Tori looked up and her eyes, brown and beady like a bird's, latched right onto mine.

They flitted to one of the empty chairs. Translation: *If you sit down, we have to be nice to you. It's the Code.*

I forced mine down into slits. Translation: *I would rather wear Kmart shoes.*

"I'm really hungry," Izzy said.

"So eat," I said. "I'm going outside to wait for my mom."

"For a half hour?"

I didn't answer her. I just whipped back through the dining hall doors, away from the "artists" and their banana sword fights, and parked myself against one of the stone pillars at the entrance until Mom got there.

Except . . . she never came.

Lunch ended. Cars arrived empty and left full of jabbering kids. A big van took some of them away. Izzy's summer sitter (she insisted on dropping the "baby" part) offered me a ride, but I said my mom was coming soon. Only I wasn't sure of that. And could I call her? No—because *I didn't have my cell phone.*

I was rehearsing the speech I was going to give my mom if she ever did show up when a small red car stopped and the passenger window rolled down. Mrs. Bernstein beckoned to me from the driver's seat.

"Hop in, Kylie," she said.

"My mom's coming," I said.

"Actually, she's not. When I saw you out here, I called her to tell her we had to lock the gate, and she said I could bring you home."

I couldn't move. I thought that was what was called being mortified.

"We can call her back if you want," Mrs. Bernstein said.

No, we weren't doing that because I was no longer speaking to my mom.

I climbed into Mrs. Bernstein's little red car, but I couldn't look at her.

I could feel her look at me, though, before she pulled through the gate. "She said she just lost track of time."

Translation: *She forgot.*

We were on the freeway before Mrs. Bernstein said anything else. The silence was all stiff until she said, "So, how did you feel about your first day?"

By that time I was so done with everything—and everybody—I said, "Do you really want to know?"

"Wouldn't have asked if I didn't."

"I'm only doing this because I have to. And to show you that I should be back on the cheerleading squad."

Actually, I hadn't thought about that until this moment. What was wrong with me? In *that* way, this was, like, the best chance ever.

I tried to copy Dad's smile before I went on. "So you can count on me to do anything you want. I'll be the best assistant ever."

For some reason, Mrs. Bernstein slid her sunglasses down her nose, looked at me over the top of them, and slid them back up again. I didn't have a translation for that.

"Here's the deal," she said when her eyes were back on the road. "I'm not even thinking about what happened with you at school. I'm focusing on those little girls. Why don't you do the same thing?"

She pulled up to the curb in front of our house, and I deflated like a balloon the day after Valentine's. All I could do was mutter a *thanks* as I opened the car door.

Mrs. Bernstein leaned across the seat I vacated. "Oh, and Kylie?"

"Yeah?" I said.

"I think these T-shirts are pretty ugly too."

At least there was that.

Chapter Seven

Mom tried to apologize to me as I stomped up the stairs, but all I said to her was, "It's *fine*. Forget about it." I didn't want to talk to her or anybody.

Well, except Jocelyn, who was sitting cross-legged in the middle of the bed, frowning into the mirror she was holding. If I were as pretty as she was, I'd be staring at myself too, only I wouldn't be scowling like that.

"Hey," Jocelyn said. She glanced at me over the top of the mirror and added, "This can't be good."

"It's awful," I said. "I don't even want to discuss it. What are you doing?"

"Deciding if I need to have my eyebrows waxed again. You want to go with me?"

I nodded and looked under the bed for Margaret. She came to me purring. I guessed she'd forgiven me for freaking out. It wasn't her first time.

I scooped up all her black furriness and joined Jocelyn on the bed. Margaret took her usual place on my chest.

"What's going on with you, Ky?" Jocelyn said. "I know you're hating all this stuff you have to do, but you always turn that kind of thing to your advantage." She put down the mirror and squinted at me. "I'm thinking that's not all of it."

I wanted to tell her about Riannon and Heidi and what they were doing to me. I really did. But that would be like admitting I was a loser. Like I couldn't control my own friends.

"Well, if there's anything I can do to help you get out of this funk . . ." Jocelyn said.

I sat straight up, tumbling Margaret into the pillows. She gave me an indignant yellow-eyed look.

"Can you get on Instagram?" I said.

"Yeah. I have the app on my phone. Here." She tossed me her iPhone in its classy white case. "Go for it. I'm going to take a shower."

When she was gone, I locked the bedroom door, and then I took the phone to the study alcove just to be safe from discovery. Margaret followed me to the swivel chair and curled into a black donut in my lap.

It took me almost no time to find #TrueK. It might have taken me even less if my fingers hadn't been all quivery and clammy. I didn't perspire *that* much after an hour of flips and cartwheels. When I found it, I wiped my hands on my shorts.

A lot of good it did me.

As soon as I saw the pictures, I broke out into a sweat so cold I shivered. And the shivers turned to shakes. And the shakes made me squeeze Margaret against me so I wouldn't cry. Because I never cried.

All the pictures—twenty of them—were of me. Doing a stag leap. Practicing a head stand. Putting on my lip gloss. Sleeping at one of our slumber parties. Only, they weren't really me. Every one of them had been changed so that I looked like an uncoordinated mess in my stag leap. In the headstand, there were huge boobs that hung upside down to my chin. Lip gloss went out to my ears. In my sleep, long strings of green snot trailed out of my nose.

How could they do this?

I knew how they did it. They had photoshopped the pictures. I knew that because I'd done it myself before. I was the one who taught Riannon and Heidi and Izzy how to do it.

That wasn't the question my wee voice was asking.

How could they do this to me? *I thought they were my friends.*

I hugged Margaret against me until she let out a meow-cry. When I loosened my arms, she didn't scramble away. She stared up at me with blinky eyes that said, *Does it hurt?*

Did a knife stabbing you in the heart hurt? It did. It hurt so much I could barely breathe.

I couldn't let that be. I didn't know how to do hurt like that. The last time my heart broke in half, I got a kitten. But right now even Kitty Margaret couldn't take away how bad and deep and terrible this felt.

So I did the only thing I knew how to do. I got mad.

I fumbled through Jocelyn's phone until I found a picture she'd taken of Heidi and Riannon and me when Heidi got her ears pierced. Perfect. Heidi had her eyes squeezed shut and her mouth in a knot while Riannon and I held her hands on either side. I cropped myself out—made Riannon's mouth super big so she looked like she was loving Heidi's pain—and I was just about to type in the caption: *Do you really believe these liars who just like to hurt people?* when someone said, "What are you doing with that phone?"

Whether it was the shock or the sweat on my hands that made

me drop it on the floor, I didn't know. I did know that my mother's pinched-in forehead meant: *I'm about to start screaming, and it may never end.*

"How did you get in here?" I said.

The diversion tactic didn't work.

"What's it going to take for you to get it?" Mom said. "Are you trying to sabotage every chance they give you?"

"I told her she could use my phone," Jocelyn said from the bathroom doorway, wrapped in a towel.

"You're not her mother," Mom said.

"Sometimes I feel like I am. I spend more time with her."

Jocelyn was better at diversion than I was. They got into an argument that gave me a chance to grab Margaret and escape to the back deck where I stayed until the yelling was over. Then Jocelyn went out, and Mom went out. Later Dad asked me if I'd had dinner, and I said yes even though I hadn't. Then I watched reality TV until my brain turned off.

∾

The next day at camp, I didn't focus on Tori and the others for two reasons.

One was that in our class, Mrs. Bernstein showed the whole group a really simple combination and divided them in half so Izzy and I could work with them on it. She stuck me with Attitude Abigail, Xerox Nichole, and Felicity of the Bare Belly. Today the too-short T-shirt had a picture of Merida on it. The girl must be obsessed with Disney princesses.

Attitude did nothing I told her to and made up her own—and, can I just say, incredibly lame—routine. Xerox copied her. Felicity tried to do *everything* I told her to, but she fell down twice and ended up with the waistband of her skirt hugging her thighs. So when we came back together to show Mrs. Bernstein—whom the other little girls were calling "Milady"—my group looked like I'd gone out for a soda break the whole time and not taught them a thing. Izzy's Callie and Daniella and Pilar had it down, and Pilar couldn't even speak English.

So that was the first reason I didn't even think about Tori or Ophelia or any of them, even when we went into the dining hall and had lunch with our "dancers." It wasn't the way second graders slurp spaghetti that kept me distracted.

It was the Instagram pictures.

Now that I had time to think, that was all I could see with that eye that's in my mind. Forty people—maybe more by now—were seeing those twisted photos of me and thinking I was some monster or something. I wanted to stand up and scream, *I'm not a bad person! Even Lydia says so!*

But who would care?

∾

Mom was late picking me up, just like she'd been late getting me there that morning, so Lydia arrived at our house just minutes after we did. Mom followed us into the library and looked down at Lydia with that pinched thing going on between her eyebrows. It seemed even more pinchy today because she had her hair pulled up so tight into its messy bun.

"Whatever you're doing, it isn't working," she said.

And then, even though she hadn't said another word to me about it since it happened, she told Lydia about me getting onto Jocelyn's phone and trying to morph pictures on Instagram. She must have been standing over me longer than I thought.

She ended the whole thing with, "We're holding up our end of this arrangement. I suggest you hold up yours."

Lydia didn't even blink. She climbed into her chair and looked at Mom eye to eye and said, "May I ask what the consequences were for Kylie?"

"Excuse me?" Mom said.

"What consequences did you give Kylie for being on the phone when you'd told her not to?"

Mom stared like Lydia was making up her own language.

"Let's have coffee this week," Lydia said.

That was it. And Mom got a look I'd never seen on her before because nobody surprised my mom.

Mom left, still looking like she'd just gotten off a carnival ride, and Lydia nodded toward the chair I'd sat in Monday. I took a different one. Then I wondered why, but it was too late to move because Lydia was already talking. At least she wasn't pulling anything out of that red bag.

"The Instagram thing," Lydia said. "Why'd you do it?"

There was no point in not answering. Not after what I just saw her pull off with my mom.

"Because they did it to me, and I was mad, so I retaliated."

Lydia nodded the enormous head of curls. The hotter it was outside, the bigger the hair seemed to get.

"You were angry."

I skipped the being hurt part and said, "Yes."

"Feelings are okay," she said. "In fact, they're good because they tell us what's going on with us. But actions based on those feelings that hurt people are not okay."

"But they tried to hurt me first," I said.

"So they control you."

"No, they don't!"

Lydia looked at me. Oh yeah. I was yelling.

"So what am I supposed to do?" I asked in a lower voice. "Just take that stuff from them?"

"That's not what I'm saying. But first of all, there's a guideline about using the Internet: don't send a message when you're angry. It never ends well."

I almost looked over my shoulder to see if a grown-up had come in. That was the way she was talking to me.

"Let me ask you this," Lydia went on. "Do you see now how Ginger felt when you did this same kind of thing to her?"

I couldn't deny I'd done that to Ginger. But there was no way I *felt* the same way she did. I just had to scramble to figure out why.

"We weren't trying to mess up Ginger's life," I said, "because she didn't really have one. But I did have one, and everyone's trying to make sure I don't get it back."

"Do you want your old life back?"

"Yes."

"Really." I could actually see her breathing in through her nose. "Okay, let's say you can't get it back. Just hypothetically."

"That means this isn't for real. We're just imagining, right?"

"Right," she said. "If you couldn't get your old life back, who would you be friends with, just because you like and respect them?"

I felt squirmy. "I don't *know*."

I don't know how to do this!

"What does this have to do with my social studies project?" I asked, louder than I meant to. I meant to be cool. I meant for her not to get to me.

70

"It has everything to do with it," Lydia said. "Do you have your assignment I gave you last time?"

"What assignment?"

"What do you do to stay popular?"

"Oh." I lowered my face so I could watch my hair fall over my eye. "I didn't write it down because it's in my head."

"Will you be sharing?" Lydia's voice was dry. Kind of like Jocelyn's sometimes.

"I'm popular because—and not to sound conceited or anything—people just want to be around me. They want to be in my group."

"I see." Lydia studied her folded hands. "I recall you telling me you have to get an *A* in everything."

"I do."

"From now on, then, you need to write out your assignments, no matter how short your answer is."

"I didn't know that was a real assignment."

"Now you do, and here's your second one." She leaned forward and looked until I had to look back at her. "You had rules for your clique, yes?"

"It wasn't a *clique*." That called for an eye roll.

"You disagree with that terminology."

"If you mean I think it's totally the wrong word, then yes."

"All right." She gave a quick nod that jostled the curls. "In the future, if you disagree with something, just say, 'I'm going to have to disagree with you there.'"

"I did say that. Sort of."

"No. You tried to make me feel like I was a clueless outsider who doesn't know a venti from a grande at Starbucks." Lydia rolled *her* eyes. "I mean, how could I *say* such a stupid thing?"

I almost laughed.

Sorry I'm Not Sorry

"Okay, I get it," I said. "Sorry."

"Are you?"

"Um . . . not really."

"Then don't say that again until you mean it. Now, back to the assignment." She leaned back now and made a steeple with her fingers under her chin. "Let's call them guidelines for your group of friends. Write them down. For next time, which will be a week from today. We won't meet Monday."

"Okay," I said.

Because what else was there to say?

Chapter Eight

I was hard to find time to do the assignment because the next week at camp made me feel like I was going down a drain.

Mrs. Bernstein kept making me work with Felicity and Attitude and Xerox for at least thirty minutes out of the two hours. Every. Single. Day. If Attitude hadn't been there, Xerox probably would have cooperated, and she actually picked up moves better than her evil little BFF when she forgot to copy *her* and copied me or Mrs. Bernstein. That happened for about seven seconds a day.

Not only that, but Attitude was just . . . rude. Like Monday—when I was in an even worse place since I had to wear the brown T-shirt—I was outside the studio with my three because Milady—they even had me calling her that—was marking out the floor for something. I was trying to get them to walk like ballerinas, and, as usual, Felicity was studying me and mouthing my words while she held her arms in a *V* instead of in a circle.

And, as usual, Attitude was doing original jazz choreography in the corner.

"Okay, just stop," I said. "Everybody. Stop."

Felicity and even Xerox did. Attitude Abby just kept flailing herself around.

"Hello-o-o-o," I said.

Attitude planted her feet and put her hands on the hips she didn't even have and said, "You're not the boss of me."

"Who even says that anymore?" I said.

"But you're not."

"Right now she is."

I turned around to see Mitch standing behind me, wearing the same brown T-shirt I was. Whoever thought the two of *us* would dress alike? It struck me that she must have grown two inches since school.

When I looked back at my group, Felicity was trying to yank her *Little Mermaid* T-shirt over her belly, and Xerox was staring like Mitch was the principal. Only Attitude lifted her chin. Translation: *Bring it.*

"She's the teacher while you're here," Mitch said. "You should respect her."

That was the most I'd ever heard Michelle Iann say at one time. And, uh, since when did I need her help? Or anybody's?

"I don't have to." Attitude cut her eyes sideways. "You can't make me."

"Don't want to make you," Mitch said. And then she just stood there looking big.

"I've got this," I said to Mitch.

She nodded and made some kind of grunting sound and walked away.

"We're going to do this again," I said to my trio.

"Bravo!" Felicity said.

"Okay," Xerox said. She was still watching Mitch go off down the path.

They both did it. Well, Xerox did. Felicity tried hard. Attitude stood there curling her lip. Two out of three was better. But still—how come Mitch thought I couldn't handle it? The G.G.s were getting pretty full of themselves.

Then when we came back together to show what we'd done, of course Izzy's group was almost perfect. I mean, as perfect as little girls with no rhythm and with legs up to their ears are going to be. Izzy didn't let me forget it.

"Aren't they just so cute?" she said Tuesday on our way to the dining hall after yet another demonstration of how far superior her group was to mine. "They do everything I say, and it's just so adorbs."

"Adorbs," I said.

I would have stopped talking to Izzy completely, but she was my only link to what was going on with Heidi and Riannon and Instagram. A whole lot of good that did me, really. Although Izzy had her phone with her every day so she could take pictures of "her" dancers—at that point my parents were the only ones who hadn't given in on the phone thing—she wouldn't show me anything on Instagram. All I could get out of her were things like:

"Sorry, Kylie, but everybody's starting to believe you're the Mean Girl poster child. Except *me*."

And: "The pictures are getting worse, but I'm not going to show them to you because I'm a better friend than that."

And: "Even the boys are in on it. Andrew and Patrick. And your Douglas."

As much as I wanted to snatch the phone from her and find out for myself, I didn't push it. Milady or Sir Devon would probably see me with it and tell Mrs. Yeats or Lydia. Besides, I couldn't forget that

I was trying to get Mrs. Bernstein to realize she needed me back on the squad. I had to wonder though: How did I get to be the girl who worried about getting into trouble?

On top of all of that, no matter how hard I tried to focus on six-year-olds talking with their mouths full of macaroni and cheese at the lunch table, I was always aware that Tori and Ophelia and Ginger and all of them were over there laughing and leaning their heads together until their hair touched and then laughing again. What could be so funny to them? I even asked Izzy that.

"I don't want to hurt your feelings," she whispered back, eyes round. "But I think they're laughing at you. They might act like they're all nice and everything, but . . ."

Izzy darted her shiny-penny eyes toward our girls, but they were all involved in a blowing-bubbles-in-your-milk contest, except Attitude, who was above all that.

Izzy put her lips closer to my ear. "I've heard them talking."

I don't want to know. I don't want to know!

"Do you want me to tell you what they said?" Izzy whispered.

"No," I said. "I don't."

"Fine." Izzy turned to the girls. "Abigail is the only one with any manners at this table."

Before I could lose my mind and pour a glass of milk over her head, I got up and said, "We're going to need more napkins."

The quickest way to get from there to the stand where the napkins were was to go past the teaching assistants' table. I could snake all through the other tables and take the long route, but I'd kind of lied to Izzy. I did want to hear what they were saying about me.

I rushed past them on the way, grabbed enough napkins to mop up the entire floor of the dining hall, and pretended to be counting them on the way back so that my slower steps wouldn't make it look like I was trying to hear the G.G.s.

It wasn't *hard* to hear them. Ginger could still sound like she was talking through one of those portable loud speakers coaches used. In fact, I didn't have to see any of them to tell who was speaking. I knew those voices.

"I've read the whole thing six times," Ginger said. "I practically know it all by heart."

"How did you *do* that?" Tori said. "I tried just reading *The Hobbit*, and I was like, 'What?'"

"You should let Ginger read it to you," Ophelia said. "It's way better."

"That's it," Shelby said. "*Lord of the Rings* sleepover at my house this weekend. I'll ask my mom."

"Should we come in costume?" Ophelia said. "I think we should come in costume. Winnie, you could be Sam. I always think of you as Sam . . ."

I didn't linger to find out what parts she gave everybody else. I didn't even stay at my table after I dumped off the napkins. I just went outside and sat on one of the stone walls and let it sink in that they weren't talking about me at all. And somehow that felt worse than it would if they'd been dissing me down to the bone.

By Thursday I was a bottle of steam. The week at camp. Mom having coffee with Lydia Wednesday and not telling me anything. Dad trying to get back on my good side and giving up after the first try, which was to bring me a teddy bear in a cheerleading outfit. A teddy bear? Really? Had he *met* me?

Yeah, that steam was ready to blow. I had to give Lydia credit because the minute I walked into the library where she was already enthroned on her seat (because I had to go to my room and get my homework first), she said, "You're looking a little like a tea kettle, Kylie. What's put you on the burner?"

It didn't surprise me anymore that she read my mind. It had to be a dwarf thing.

"Everything," I said.

"Name one thing."

What could I tell her that was safe?

No one likes me anymore.

"There's this kid in my group at camp," I said. "She's, like, the biggest brat I ever met."

"How so?"

"I'm supposed to be helping her with the routine, and she just talks back or ignores me and she's got, like, the smartest mouth."

"So, she's a trigger."

"She's a pain in the butt!"

Lydia grinned. "No, I mean she triggers your anger. Like a finger on a gun—she makes it go off." The grin left. "If you let her."

"I haven't blown up at her yet," I said.

"Good. And I'm going to help you so you never will. For starters, between now and Monday I want you to make a list of all the things that trigger you."

"Is that a real assignment?" I said.

"Yes, that's a real assignment. Speaking of which . . ."

Her gaze floated down to my paper on the table. Without meaning to, I covered it with my hand.

"Problem?" Lydia said.

Yes, all of a sudden there was. I'd written my guidelines that I expected my friends to follow and had Jocelyn type them since I wasn't allowed on the computer, and I'd even signed the paper at the bottom in a signature I practiced five times on a piece of scratch paper to find the best one.

But when I had to show them to Lydia, I felt heat rushing into my face, and I knew I was turning the color of her gigantic bag. Only I wasn't mad.

I'm embarrassed.

And that just didn't happen.

"I don't need to read them unless you want me to," Lydia said. "I just need to make sure you did the assignment."

"Why don't you need to read them?" I asked.

"Because it was mostly for you. Call it preparation for your project, which I think I can put together for you now."

If I hadn't been relieved, that would have been a trigger right there: me spending hours on a paper she wasn't even going to look at. Not only that, but her next words almost catapulted me from the chair:

"I have a message for you from Mrs. Yeats."

My hand jerked across the paper and sent it flying to the floor. I let it stay there. I was suddenly having trouble breathing.

Lydia went on like none of that happened. "She said to tell you she's pleased with what she's hearing about your work at the camp."

"What's she hearing?" I asked, and I didn't care how eager I sounded.

"Mr. Devon tells her that you sit with your students at lunch instead of hanging out with the other seventh graders. He says that shows some real commitment on your part."

I couldn't look at her.

"And Mrs. *Bernstein* tells her you're showing a lot of patience with your students. Apparently, one little girl in particular practically worships you."

That would be Bare-Belly Felicity. Who *didn't* the poor kid worship? So far this wasn't the news I was looking for.

Lydia folded her hands in that stack thing. "So the bottom line is, according to Mrs. Yeats, if you keep up your good work at camp and meet the other criteria, she really will reconsider her decision."

"She will?" I said. "Really?"

I was almost ready to shout, *Bravo!*

I didn't, of course.

"Really," Lydia said. "Now why don't you go ahead right now and start writing down those triggers we talked about."

∽

I would have written a five-paragraph *essay* about triggers if she'd asked me to. For the first time since I walked out of Mrs. Yeats' office, I could actually imagine myself back at Gold Country Middle, out at the edge of the football field leading the whole seventh grade in cheering our team on—and dancing out on the field at halftime—and wearing my uniform to school on pep rally days with the Jacket. And feeling special again.

I decided the first thing I had to do to keep that going was make sure our little dance team was the best. The. Best. And I could show them how. Especially when on Friday, Sir Devon told the whole camp in the Gathering Place that on Saturday, July 25, each group would be part of a big presentation for the parents and the whole community. That was all I needed to hear.

When we got to the studio, I pulled my three girls aside and ignored the fact that Attitude was perfecting her eye rolling and said to them, "Okay, dancers. You heard about the big presentation."

"Yes!" Felicity said. "Do we get to wear tutus?"

I tried not to get an image of her bare belly bulging from a froth of tulle and was about to go on when Attitude let out a giant snort.

"Hairball?" I said.

"You can't wear a tutu," she said to Felicity. "You're too fat."

I stared at her. I would have stared at her longer if Felicity hadn't burst into full-out crying.

"Is something wrong over there?" Milady asked from across the room.

Ya think?

I shook my head at her. I kind of wanted to handle it myself. Actually, I kind of wanted to drag Attitude out of there by her curly little mop. But I thought of another mop of curly hair, around a face that was telling me Attitude was a trigger and she could only make me pull it if I let her.

"Abigail," I forced myself to say, "that was rude."

"Sor-ry," she said.

Please, please, please don't let me smack her.

"Do you actually mean that?" I said.

Attitude lifted her chin and shook her head.

"Then don't say it until you do."

Attitude Abby looked like she'd just tripped over something.

All that time, Xerox was jiggling like somebody waiting in line for the restroom, afraid she wasn't going to make it. Felicity was sniffing up tears and snot, but at least she wasn't bawling out loud. Shouldn't I do something, though?

"Hey," I said to her. "You're not really that fat. You just wear shirts that are too small."

She just sort of blinked at me. Okay, maybe that wasn't it.

Chapter Nine

My plan for whipping my little dancers into shape was going to have to start with me getting to camp on time. Mom had made me late almost every single day because she was either talking on the phone, texting on the phone, or looking something up on the phone. I hardly ever saw her face without a rectangle in the middle of it.

Sunday night I told her about twelve times that we should leave at seven thirty to get there by eight. So Monday morning I was almost purple in the face when I got all dressed and blow-dried and lip glossed, only to find her still in her pajamas in the breakfast nook, drinking coffee and *texting somebody*.

I knew if I opened my mouth I was going to spew out the fit of the century, so instead I marched back upstairs and shook Jocelyn. Margaret looked at me like I was nuts, which I probably was, because Jocelyn was even less of a morning person than me. As in, touch her before she woke up on her own and you were likely to draw back a nub.

She spared me the amputation of my hand, but the look she gave me was enough to scald off my face.

"Will you please, please take me to camp?" I said.

"Where's Mom?" I thought she said, although it came out more like, "Phma phawm?"

"Downstairs in her pajamas still, and it's time to go."

"Where's Dad?"

"I don't know. I'm not talking to Dad."

"Good." Her eyes came unstuck. "Okay, I'll take you."

She did, without even stopping to pee or get dressed. She just drove me in her Beamer, wearing sleep pants and a cami. She wasn't talking much yet, but I was okay with that. I was dealing with a head full of straight-up steam.

When we got to the gate and I was opening the car door, Jocelyn said, "Don't let Mom get to you like that. She's not going to change, so it isn't worth it."

I nodded and got out. But as she drove away, I realized something: Mom must be one of my triggers.

I can't wait to tell Lydia.

It must have been my day for *Oh, yeah, huh?* moments because I had another one during class. It had actually been brewing for a while, but it really boiled over that day.

I was working on making pretty pliés with my three dancers, and Xerox got it right away.

"That's what we're lookin' for," I told her and turned to Felicity. "You can totally do this too. Stand right behind Xe—Nichole—and pretend you're her shadow."

Felicity giggled.

"Come on, you can do it," Nichole said.

That surprised me. It clearly *shocked* Attitude because she said, "Nicky, don't even think about doing that."

The words weren't any different from what she'd been saying

since Day One. But in that moment, it wasn't Abigail's bossy voice I was hearing or Abigail's eyes I saw bulging out like warnings at Nichole. That voice and those eyes—they were somebody else's. Somebody familiar. I just couldn't figure out whose.

"Do it, Nicky," I said.

"Her name's Nichole," Abigail said.

"But you can call me Nicky."

That was one brave little kid because Abigail's eyes turned into switchblades.

"You two—keep practicing that." I looked at Abby. "Come over to the corner with me."

"Why?" she said.

I didn't answer her because I knew I couldn't come up with anything that would end this.

She followed me to the corner and tried to do that *plant the feet, put your hands on your hips* thing, but I didn't give her a chance.

"Do you even know how to dance?" I said.

"Yes! Duh! I *told* you I started taking lessons when I was two."

"So how come I haven't seen you dance one single time since you've been here?"

"I've been dancing!"

"Not like Milady and I have asked you to."

"Your dances are dumb. I like to do it my own way."

"Is that what you tell your dance teacher at your studio?" I said.

The round little rebel face turned straight toward the floor, curls tumbling down.

"When did you quit dance lessons?" I said. "I stopped at the end of fifth grade."

Abigail stole a glance at me. "Why?"

I took a deep breath. I was about to say something I'd never told anybody before, and I was going to tell it to this little kid who would probably backtalk me until I graduated from high school.

"I quit because I didn't like the teacher telling me what to do," I said. "And I was afraid if I tried to do what she said, she'd tell me it was wrong. And I didn't like to be wrong."

As soon as it was out, I wondered whether I'd just lost it. All I could do now was wait and find out.

"Are you sorry?" she said.

"Sorry about what?" I said.

"Are you sorry you quit because of that?"

I didn't even have to think about it. "Every single day," I said.

It was like somebody flipped Abigail's On switch. When we did our pretty pliés and walked in a circle like perfect ballerinas and leapt across the space, she was like a junior Jocelyn.

I would have been digging it if Nicky didn't all of a sudden grow a third foot or something. It seemed like the better Abigail was, the less Nicky knew how to do.

Before I could even say, *Hellooo . . . you just had this!* Abigail jumped her little self in front of Nicky and did it all wrong, exactly the way Nicky was doing it wrong.

Felicity completely stopped and gaped at both of them with her mouth halfway open. I couldn't blame her. Abigail was making fun of her own friend, the only girl in the whole camp who could even stand her.

Milady clapped her hands. "All right, dancers, let's come back together."

Nicky bolted for the circle, and Felicity wasn't far behind her—or she would have been if her skirt hadn't gotten caught in her ballet slipper. I had to stop and help her before she ended up half naked, so I couldn't talk to Attitude about what just went down.

I wasn't sure what I would have said to her anyway.

The good news was that when Milady got everyone into formation and turned on the music, the performance almost looked like all six of them knew the same dance. Abigail practically looked like she was for the *Nutcracker*, and Felicity got through it without being a danger to herself or others. I would actually have been impressed . . . if Nicky didn't do the whole thing like she was going to be grounded if she made the wrong move. At the end, when Felicity led the group in an endless series of *Bravos*, Nicky ran off to the bathroom.

I watched her retreat with her shoulders already shaking and her weird-angled hair jerking up and down.

I should go after her.

But I wouldn't have a clue what to say.

Still, I was excited, which was a new thing for me. I'd watched girls like Ophelia get all squealy about, like, science projects, and that just didn't seem cool to me. Usually, there wasn't much to get all that jazzed about. Even cheerleading, which was my reason for living, didn't make me go . . . well . . . *Bravo!*

But seeing those little girls finally getting it, having the chance to show Mrs. Bernstein and everybody that I was great at this, and showing the camp that our group was the best—that seemed kind of huge to me. I even felt tingly, like I'd just used Jocelyn's apricot scrub, only on the inside.

What was weird was that I was kind of looking forward to telling Lydia about my plan. When I did lay it out for her, though, I left out the tingly part. I only discussed that with Margaret.

"This is progress," Lydia said when I was through. "I like seeing you get enthused about something."

She was smiling. The curls were nodding. So why did it sound like any minute there was going to be a 'but'?

I pressed the back of my head against the chair. "*Now* what did I say wrong?"

"I'm sorry?"

"You want me to find something I like and I do, and then you're just, 'Oh, that's nice.'"

Lydia grinned. "Were you expecting a parade, Kylie?"

"No." I folded my arms and then refolded them.

"Okay," Lydia said. "You're pretty perceptive, so let's go ahead and go there."

"Go where?"

"Shall we have some tea?"

Everything in me stopped.

Tea? That makes me think of—

I didn't want to think about it, but I could already see it. I was *there.* Sitting at the small round table in a pool of sunshine in my room with the Peter Rabbit pot and cups only big enough for two sips. A rag doll as big as I was sitting across from me with my other chocolate chip cookie on her Cottontail plate. Margaret calling that cookie a biscuit and saying, "Would you like milk in yours, Wee One?"

"Should I take that as a *no*?" Lydia asked.

Yes. No. There was no tea in our house. Mom didn't know how to make it.

"Do you mind if I have some?" Lydia asked.

She didn't wait for me to answer but reached into the red bag—where else—and pulled out a thermos and two mugs. They had gnome faces on them that were so real I expected them to start talking.

"I'll pour you some—see if you like it," Lydia said.

She used to say that! Margaret used to say, "See if you like it—it has milk and sugar—"

I wouldn't like it. I didn't like any tea that wasn't Margaret's.

Steam curled from the cups as Lydia filled them. I waited for the gnomes to scream.

"I like to improve the moment," Lydia said and pushed one of the mugs toward me.

Tea makes everything better. She always said that—

Lydia took a sip and closed her eyes and stroked the gnome's nose with her finger. I couldn't even reach for my mug. It didn't have Tom Kitten on it.

He was my favorite.

"Now," she said when all that was done, "you wanting to show Mrs. Bernstein that you can be trusted is awesome. You wanting to help make your group the best it can be . . . double awesome." She took another sip, face wrinkling in the heat. "What isn't so awesome is you wanting your group to be better than all the other groups."

"What's wrong with that?" I said.

"Do you have to make everyone else feel 'less than' for you to feel good about yourself?" Lydia set aside her cup. "The idea is for you to feel good because you *are* good. Not because all the other people are bad."

I opened my mouth to protest. I was even going to say, *I have to disagree with you.*

But Lydia pushed my mug closer to me and said, "That's one of those things you can't really argue with, Kylie. It's up there with 'you may do bad things, but you aren't a bad person.' Try the tea."

I want to. I want tea again. Margaret said it made everything better.

I picked up the mug and blew into it until the liquid wrinkled. It was creamy-looking, just the way Margaret always said it should be. When I tasted it . . . honey . . . hot milk . . . smooth as hot licorice.

Lady Grey. My favorite.

We sipped without talking for a few minutes. The only sound was the tick of the clock the housekeeper wound every week but no one ever looked at.

"How are you doing with your triggers?" Lydia asked.

"I found some," I said.

"Good. I think you are ready for another card."

I drained my mug and set it down with the gnome facing me. "I have to disagree with you there," I said to it.

"Nicely put," Lydia said. "Tell me some more."

"The card thing. I'm so not gonna walk around with them in my pocket."

"No one said you had to. Keep them wherever you want to."

Why did I hardly ever have a comeback for her?

"I have a new one for you," she said.

Again with the bag. This time she pulled out a card that said, *Consider your smudge* in brown letters.

"You ever read the Bible, Kylie?" Lydia asked as she slid the card across the table toward me.

Did she wake up this morning and decide this was the day to torture me with memories?

"Not by myself," I said.

Margaret used to read me the stories.

Lydia's eyebrows went up, but she went on. "Did anyone ever tell you the part about wiping the smudge off your own face before you point out the speck of dirt on somebody else's?"

"Is that like the log in your eye?" I asked.

"That's the one. You have a head start on it."

"How?"

"When you told Little Miss Attitude you quit dance lessons too, you helped her instead of putting her down."

"I wanted to flush her down the toilet."

"But you didn't. So you didn't let her pull your trigger. See how this all works together?"

I had to admit I kind of did, but I still didn't see how it was going to get me—

"You're getting this, Kylie," Lydia said. "Even if you don't know it yet."

I did have to agree with her on that second part.

Chapter Ten

I still didn't get how making sure my group was the best was such a bad thing. Nobody could really stop me from doing that, right?

Um, wrong.

We were hardly settled onto our log row in the Gathering Place the next morning, Tuesday—me with Felicity pressing against me on one side and Nicky on the other so that I felt like the filling in a panini—when Sir Devon made another big announcement that was *bravo*-worthy. At least to everybody else.

"This week, artists," he said, tossing his gray ponytail like he was proclaiming victory over marauding bands of dragons, "you will begin to see how the pieces you're preparing will come together in . . ." He paused so the crowd could hold their breath and wait for it. "One big production!"

I was pretty sure the littler kids, like ours, had no idea what he was talking about, but they sprang up and cheered anyway. I stayed seated even when Felicity stomped on my feet about five times.

One big production? Everybody working together? It wasn't

going to just be one act after another, like a dance recital? Like a gymnastics competition? Like I imagined it?

"The writing group will soon give you the script for our story," he said. "Come up, scribes!"

A line of fourth graders, almost all of whom wore glasses and had braces, scrambled over log benches and joined Sir Devon on the stage. Shelby and Winnie, looking teacher-like, got them in a line. When Shelby asked, "Ready?" they all cried out, "Write on!" and waved big fluffy feathery quill pens in the air. The Gathering went nuts.

"So lame, right?" Izzy whispered to me over Nicky's stair-step hair.

Don't pull the trigger.

What trigger? I couldn't exactly put it into words, but I knew there *was* one.

"Right?"

I turned to Izzy. Her phone was in my face.

"Did you just take my picture?" I said.

"Yeah."

"Why?"

"I'm making an album of our whole summer," she said.

It was going to be an album on steroids, then. Almost all she did was take pictures. Every kid who looked at her immediately broke into this big cheesy smile. She probably had a lot of photos of gums. Tonsils even.

Anyway, just because our group was now a part of some big story Winnie and Shelby were dreaming up, and Ginger and Ophelia's people were going to act out, and the other dance class with third and fourth and fifth graders in it were going to dance too, that didn't mean *we* couldn't rock this thing. The more I thought about it, the better it sounded, actually. Our baby girlfriends could steal the show.

From whom?
I couldn't answer that.

~

I was glad Thursday that Lydia finally gave me my assignment for the social studies project. It was the only one of Mrs. Yeats' criteria thingies I hadn't met yet, and I wanted to get going on it. There was barely a month left before cheerleading practice would start. I had to be ready.

Although when Lydia presented it to me, I wasn't so sure.

First I had to study the Bill of Rights. Before she even finished saying it, I'd already decided I was going to memorize all ten amendments by Monday. She'd be impressed.

"Then I want you to look at the guidelines you put together for your group of friends," Lydia said.

What group of friends?

I squeezed my eyes shut.

"Kylie? You okay?"

"What do you want me to do with them?" I asked. I wanted her to keep talking so I couldn't hear my wee voice.

Lydia looked at me like she was curious. "I want you to decide if those guidelines are a Bill of Rights for a friendship. If they are, you're good to go. If not, you'll need to write them as one."

"As a Bill of Rights," I said.

"That's right."

I don't understand.

"Make sense?" Lydia said.

"Yes."

No!

I would figure it out. On my own.

"You already have three," Lydia said.

"I do?"

"On the Code Cards. No Rivals. Don't Pull the Trigger. Consider the Smudge."

Lydia held up all her fingers like fans. "See if you can come up with more."

Ugh. I was going to have to pull out those lame things after all.

∿

But I didn't until Sunday. Mom and Dad were having a pool party for people from Dad's law office. Mom said Jocelyn and I could each invite some friends, but Jocelyn told me it was going to be one big yawn fest . . . and I didn't have anybody to invite, except Izzy. And she had become the biggest trigger of them all.

Two days before, on Friday, we were on our way to lunch, and she tried to tell me how Riannon was growing out her hair because she was tired of being my clone and how Heidi was doing the same thing because now she was doing everything Riannon did. And how they were hanging out with Andrew and Patrick. And Douglas.

When I told Izzy I didn't want to hear anything about Riannon and Heidi, she looked at me like I'd had a face transplant.

Then she started in on how I was a better actor than Ophelia and a better writer than Winnie and a *way* better leader than Tori.

When I asked her why she was telling me all that, *her* whole face turned into one big *Huh?*

Finally, when she asked me if I had a plan to "do something about" Winnie and Shelby's script when it came, I said, "Izzy, what are you *talking* about?"

"Are we even friends anymore?" she said.

"*What?*"

By then we were standing outside the dining hall, and a bevy of ponytailed fifth grade girls in the other dance class did a pirouette toward us at the same time. I plastered on a fake smile until they all skittered into the hall. I hadn't done that in a long time.

I was letting Izzy pull my trigger.

I pulled in a long breath. "Iz," I said, "why are you asking me that?"

"Because." Izzy's cheeks were crayon red. "It's not like it used to be. I don't know. It's just weird."

Then she wriggled her round shoulders and disappeared into the dining hall.

Now as I sat on Jocelyn's bed with a copy of the Bill of Rights she printed out for me, a pad of paper, the Code Cards, and, of course, Margaret cleaning between the pink pads of her whipped cream paw, I sort of knew what Izzy was talking about.

Did I really want her as a friend?

"These Code Card things are making me weird," I said to Margaret.

I picked up the Consider the Smudge one—the one I'd doodled a big old log on, sticking out of a huge eye—and scratched her between the ears with it.

"You're doing *homework*?" Jocelyn swept across the room and tossed her Coach bag on the chair. "It's Sunday."

The skin around her eyebrows was raw-looking red. She must have just had them waxed.

"I don't have anything else to do," I said.

"That's just wrong."

Jocelyn glided onto the bed beside me and pushed at the Cards with a freshly polished nail. She must have had a manicure too. And probably a pedi.

"What are these?" she said.

I gathered Margaret into my lap. "I have to follow them if I want to get back into school."

Jocelyn looked at them closer. Then her green eyes came up to me. "For real?" she said.

I looked down at the Code Cards too. *Was* I doing it for real?

"Okay, I've gotta get you out of here," Jocelyn said. "Come on."

"Where are we going?"

"I have no idea. Just as long as it's not here."

~

Jocelyn did have an idea, of course. She always did. First the Beamer took us over to the other side of Grass Valley to get Starbucks at the drive-through.

"We're getting cake pops," she said.

"Those are for little kids," I said.

"Why should they have all the fun? Everything tastes better on a stick."

After that we went by the movie theater to see what was playing. Everything was PG-13.

"You could totally pass," Jocelyn said. "I could put some eye shadow on you."

"What about our drinks?" I said. "We can't take them in."

Jocelyn hitched her bag up on her shoulder. "That's what big purses are for." She opened the Beamer door. "You need an adventure."

Even in my flip-flops my feet felt heavy as we walked across the parking lot. The black top was so hot it sucked at my soles. Maybe that was why I could only manage to shuffle behind Jocelyn. Or maybe it was something else.

Jocelyn handed the ticket girl her debit card and turned to me.

"You're going to need one of these when I go to San Francisco. Start working on Dad."

I started to tell her I wasn't speaking to Dad, but I wasn't sure that was true. I hadn't really even seen him for days.

Jocelyn took my drink and tucked it into her bag. "You want anything else?"

Even as I was shaking my head, she led the way to the line that trailed out from the refreshment counter. I stood there hoping nobody was going to come ask me how old I was or check Jocelyn's purse for illegal iced mochas. The longer we waited, the more my stomach hurt. Why wasn't this feeling like much of an adventure?

"You want popcorn, right?" Jocelyn said.

I shook my head again. My stomach suddenly didn't like the chocolate cake pop.

"I'm going to the restroom," I said.

"I'll meet you," she said.

Everybody in Grass Valley must have decided to go to the movies that afternoon, and I had to squeeze my way through all of them to get to the girls' bathroom. I had to wonder why a bunch of *boys* would be in front of the door. Shouldn't they be over there playing video games?

I tried to squeeze between two of them, but they chose that moment to chest bump each other. I was caught like a piece of bologna in a sandwich with my face shoved into the one guy's throat. Was there a reason why guys didn't discover deodorant until long after girls did?

Holding my breath so I wouldn't gag—since I was already nauseated in the first place—I tried to wriggle free. Instead of backing off, they pressed harder. I couldn't breathe. I couldn't even yell, *Get off me!*

I *could* feel the one behind me laughing; his stomach was rippling against my back. The one in front dug his chin into my head, so his throat vibrated into my face as he said, "Did you get it?"

Wait. I knew that voice. I wrenched my arms free and pushed at his shoulders. Patrick O'Connor looked down at me with his mouth wide open. When did he get to be so tall? And when did he become a gorilla?

"What are you *doing*, Patrick?" I said.

"Anything I want," he said.

He took a step forward and backed me into the other kid, who blew his hot breath next to my ear.

"You weren't thinking you were going to go in the bathroom, were you?"

Douglas. The Douglas who said he liked me.

"Hey, Patrick, she has to go to the bathroom," he said.

"Too bad," Patrick said. "'Cause that bathroom's not for lying traitors."

He moved closer like he was going to trap me again, but I knew something about Patrick. I poked him in the rib with one finger, and he squealed like a little girl.

I didn't feel I'd won, though, as I squirmed away from them and escaped into the bathroom. Even if I had, it wouldn't have lasted long. The place was empty, except for two girls standing at the sinks.

Riannon and Heidi.

The room spun the way it does when you do too many turns without spotting yourself. When it stopped, I wasn't sure it was Heidi and Riannon I was looking at. Riannon was pointier than I remembered her, maybe because her hair was longer, just like Izzy said, and she had it pulled straight back from her face. Heidi's hair had grown some too, and I saw dark roots from the highlights she had put in last spring. Her turned-up nose wasn't so cute now, maybe because it was

NANCY RUE

wrinkled as if she smelled something bad . . . and that something
was me.

"How did she get in here?" Riannon said to Heidi.

"Yeah, we had guards," Heidi said.

You had two big apes, I wanted to say, but the words wouldn't come
out. I felt like something was strangling me.

Riannon kept her phony-green eyes beaded on Heidi. "Tell her
she needs to leave."

Heidi tossed her shaggy bangs out of her eyes. "I'm not talking
to her."

"Maybe she'll go if she hears us saying she's invisible to us now."

"Who?" Heidi said.

She gave her snorty laugh. Riannon just curled her lip until I
could see her gums.

The bathroom door swung open, and both of them whipped their
faces back to the mirror.

"Excuse me, honey," a lady said behind me.

I managed to move like a stick to get out of her way. When she
went into a stall, I faced the mirror too.

It used to be when I looked at my two best friends, it was like seeing my own reflection. But right now, with my face between theirs in
the glass, I was pale and my skin pulled across my cheekbones and
my eyes were big and confused. I didn't look like me.

And I didn't look like them.

"Ready to go, Heidi?" Riannon said.

But I was out the door before they could even turn around.

Jocelyn was standing in the hallway, calmly munching popcorn
while nobody *older than* thirteen swarmed around her. When she saw
me, she jerked her head toward the theaters, but I shook mine and
darted through the crowd for the front door.

She was way too cool to yell after me. She only yelled at Mom and Dad. Even when she caught up to me outside, her voice was steady.

"Are you okay?" she said.

"I'm sick," I said. And that wasn't a lie.

I'd never felt worse in my life.

Chapter Eleven

I went to bed as soon as we got home, and I stayed there until the next morning. It wasn't that hard to do with Mom and Dad being all about their party and Jocelyn guarding me better than the two Gorilla Boys at the theater. She said she was sure it was the cake pop and the double chocolate iced mocha and the whipped cream that were making me pale as a mime, but the way she looked at me, I think she knew it was something else.

I would have *kept* staying in bed the next morning, but for one thing, I was tired of seeing Riannon and Heidi in my head like those weird reflections you make in mirrors at the fair. And for another thing, I couldn't miss a day of camp.

Jocelyn dropped me off with an Egg McMuffin I couldn't eat still in my hand. The van had just delivered a bunch of kids, and as I trudged toward the Gathering Place, one of them broke free from the pack and nudged her head under my elbow. When I looked down, Felicity was snuggling into me.

"Um, hi," I said.

"Hi! Guess what?"

"What?"

I sort of wanted to pull away because her whole body was damp, but she was latched on.

"I practiced the whole weekend!"

"For?"

"For our dance, silly! Wanna see?"

Before I could even think about answering, Felicity dropped her backpack, stood in the starting position for our routine, and closed her eyes like she was seeing the whole thing. And then she *did* the whole thing, there in the parking lot, with no music except what was obviously playing in her head.

When she was done, her face was strawberry-colored and her hair was plastered to the sides of her head, but the smile . . . it sparkled into her eyes.

"Ohmygosh, Felicity," I said.

"It was good?"

"It was awesome."

"Are we having an impromptu rehearsal?"

That was Milady Bernstein, still putting her lanyard around her neck as she walked toward us.

"Did you see her?" I said.

"I did." Milady lifted her chin at Felicity and smiled. "Did you take some extra lessons over the weekend?"

"No," I said. "She just practiced. It's, like, a miracle."

Felicity shook her head so hard I actually felt some droplets on my arm. "I just closed my eyes, and I saw Lady Kylie teaching me and then I did it."

Something thick started happening in my throat.

Lady Kylie. I love that.

"Then I think there's only one thing to do," Mrs. Bernstein said, more to me than to Felicity. "We need to let Lady Kylie teach the class today."

Felicity did a happy dance that was nothing like the one I'd taught her and took off toward the Gathering Place with her backpack bouncing behind her.

"I just realized something, Kylie," Mrs. Bernstein said. "That's the first time I've ever heard you talk about another girl without . . ." She shook her head like she'd just changed her mind about something. "You were positive. I like it." Her chin went up again, this time at my Egg McMuffin. "Breakfast?"

I nodded, but when we passed the trash can, I tossed it in. I wasn't hungry, but not because I was sick.

I was excited again.

∽

Although Izzy didn't talk to me when we got to the studio that morning, and she stiffened up like somebody had sprayed her with starch when Milady said I would be leading the class, she still took pictures. More than ever, in fact. I didn't pay that much attention though.

I had a class to teach. And my students were ah-mazing. Even if there were bellies showing and clumps of hair sticking to sweaty faces and giggles erupting every minute. They listened. They followed. They remembered. Attitude didn't roll her eyes one time. They were actually starting to look like small versions of dancers.

They're Wee Dancers.

I liked that. Even if it did give me the Missing Margaret feeling.

It was going so well until Winnie brought in the script for the camp production, a spiral-bound booklet all decorated with damsels and knights and dragons. I dropped back to the edge of our half-moon circle and watched my dancers go beyond squealing. The drawings blew their little minds more than the thought of tutus. I could feel my face tightening in a way it hadn't done in a while.

Then when Winnie told the story, even her pale voice riveted them to their places on the floor. Any minute they were going to start calling her Lady Winnie. My teeth clenched.

The play was filled with lords and ladies and *alases* and *forsooths*, and I wasn't even sure the kids understood it all. But when Winnie stopped and said, "This is the part where you'll come onstage and do your dance you've been learning," every one of them was up on her knees, little hands clasped, craning her neck to see. If anyone was breathing, I'd be surprised. My own breathing came in hard puffs. Really? Winnie was their idol now?

"You'll be Princess Genevieve's ladies-in-waiting," Winnie said.

All the Wee Dancers gasped at once. Abigail's hand shot up, although the question was out of her mouth before Winnie even called on her.

"What's a lady-in-waiting?" she said.

Winnie paused—long enough for Abigail to get frustrated. She hadn't made *that* much progress. We weren't expecting a personality transplant.

Attitude Abby whipped her head back toward me.

"We don't even know what a lady-in-waiting *is*," she said.

I did know. Jocelyn and I had just watched an old musical called *Camelot* a couple of weeks before, the kind of thing that came on after midnight when nobody was watching.

So I could've told Abigail and shown Winnie these were *my* girls, and even though they might think she was all that right now, they would forget about her the minute she left because *I* was their Lady

Kylie. I hate to admit I actually would have done it if wee voice hadn't whispered . . .

I'm sick of being jealous.

Attitude was still looking at me. Winnie was still pausing. Milady Bernstein was starting to get to her feet.

"Do I look like I know?" I asked. "Ask her. Winnie."

The little heads whipped back around. Winnie's normally all-white face turned pink, as if the sun was rising on it.

"They're very important people," she said. "They make sure the princess has everything she needs."

"Sort of like slaves," Izzy said.

I opened my mouth to tell Izzy she was an idiot, but Milady Bernstein glared her down with a sharp look I hadn't seen all summer and asked Winnie to go on with the story. She did, but first she looked at me and gave me a mini-smile. Translation: *Thanks*, maybe? I shrugged. Translation: *It's your gig.*

When Winnie left, it took us twenty minutes to get the girls all settled down again. I was a little bit jazzed myself. Knowing how we fit into the whole production was going to make it fun to add some cool touches to our dance. Milady Bernstein agreed. Izzy was basically pouting. As for the Wee Dancers, they already moved more like members of the royal court than little girls just doing a dance. Did they totally get who ladies-in-waiting were? Probably not. But Felicity was sure that meant she was going to get to wear a tutu.

I looked at Attitude Abby to make sure she wasn't going to tell Felicity she'd never fit in one. But Abigail was in the corner, practicing her pliés.

～

When I told Lydia about it that afternoon, she got a grin on her face as big as a slice of watermelon and said, "Now you're finding out what happy really is."

I wish that were true.

But it wasn't. She didn't know what happened at the movies. I didn't tell her. When I wasn't meeting with Lydia or teaching my Wee Dancers or standing up in the Gathering Place and yelling, "Bravo!" I was seeing Heidi and Riannon's faces in the mirror of my mind. I couldn't erase them because now I knew . . . it wasn't their moms who turned them against me . . . they weren't pretending to hate me so they could get back into school and cheerleading . . . they really did hate me, and they were making sure everyone else did too. Including Douglas and all the who-knew-how-many people they were reaching on Instagram with their ugly, made-up pictures of me.

It hurts, it hurts, it hurts! the wee voice cried out every time I got quiet and still.

So for the next two days, I tried never to be quiet and still.

I memorized all ten amendments in the Bill of Rights. I also re-read my guidelines for my so-called friends, which made me feel like I'd turned on a heating pad inside my face.

1. Don't invite anybody else to our table or our parties or anything without asking the rest of the posse.
2. Report to the group anything bad you hear people saying about any of us.
3. Don't come to school looking like a mess. Like in track pants or a sweatshirt.
4. Keep your cell phone on all the time so we can contact one another.
5. *Always keep the group's secrets.*

I was glad now that Lydia had never looked at them. I was definitely going to have to do the assignment: Create a bill of rights for friendship because what I'd written down wasn't like the right to free speech or any of those. Actually, it was kind of the opposite.

First, though, I decided to get rid of my old rules so nobody would see them. Especially Lydia. Wednesday afternoon I took the paper into Dad's study and put it through his shredder.

"Where have you been, princess?"

I, like, had a convulsion and whirled around to see Dad's tall self in the doorway. What was with my parents being able to sneak up on me? That never used to happen.

He kissed me on the side of my head and kept going to his desk. He had a stack of mail in one hand and his briefcase in the other. I could smell the leather from across the room.

"Have you been avoiding me?" he said as he started sorting the envelopes into piles, still standing up.

"Yes," I said.

"Huh. How do we end up with all this junk? So why's that?"

"Why's what?"

"Why are you avoiding me?" He picked up one envelope and glared at it like it was in big trouble.

"Because you don't listen to me when I talk anyway, so what's the point?"

I turned to go. I was actually halfway through the door before he said, "Whoa, Kylie."

I stopped, but I kept my back to him.

"You need to watch your tone."

"Sorry," I said.

And then I whirled around.

"Actually, Dad," I said, "that's wrong. I shouldn't have said I was sorry because I'm not. Maybe I should be . . . but I'm totally not."

Dad's hands went to his hips. The eyebrows were making a slow rise to his hair. "If you have something to say, princess, say it. I'm listening."

Of course, *now* I had no idea what I wanted to tell him. Maybe one thing that came to me right that very minute.

"I don't think I'm a princess anymore," I said.

And *then* I left.

That was Wednesday afternoon, which meant I had to wait twenty-four hours to talk to Lydia. Right then, she was the only person I wanted to talk to because even Kitty Margaret couldn't help me find my way out of where I was.

All day Thursday, which marked almost a month since Mrs. Yeats gave me my criteria and my world fell apart like Humpty Dumpty, I was counting the hours and then the minutes. Well, except for during lunch. During lunch, it was like being stuck in time.

I was headed to the dining hall with Felicity holding one hand with her clammy one (was the child ever dry?) and Pilar clutching the other one while she chattered away in half-Spanish-half-English when Mrs. Bernstein caught up with us.

"Lady Kylie," she said, which made both of them giggle, "I forgot to tell you that you have a production meeting at lunch."

That sounded kind of cool and official. Until I saw the look in her black eyes, which was saying, *I'm not sure you're going to like this.*

"It's with the adult teachers and all the assistants—back at the faculty table."

I didn't care if it was at Disneyland; I didn't want to go. She had that part right.

All those triggers will be there.

No *doubt*.

"We'll have a chance to tell them our ideas for the show," Mrs. Bernstein said. "And I want you to speak up because you have some good ones."

Felicity was tugging at my hand, pulling me toward the door. She was never one to want to be late for a meal.

"What about the girls? I always sit with them."

"They'll be fine. Felicity, you and Pilar go on."

Felicity didn't say *Bravo!* to that, but she let go of my hand and followed Pilar, although she looked back three times as if she was afraid I was going to disappear.

"These girls love you," Mrs. Bernstein said.

Then they're the only ones.

I swallowed. Hard. No way I was going into this meeting with a thick throat.

As I trailed Mrs. Bernstein to the back table, wishing I would suddenly come down with acute appendicitis, I had a weird thought: *I wonder if there's a card I should be using here.*

They all ran together in my head. Consider the smudge don't pull the trigger there are no rivals.

I needed all of them.

Everybody else was there when we got to the table, which was really two pushed together to get everybody in. I didn't know the other grown-ups except Mr. Devon. They all sat at one end, and the assistants were at the other. I knew all of *them*, including the eighth grade girl with hair streaked like my mom's who was helping with the older dance class. Her name was Vanessa, and she was a cheerleader too. She barely looked at me as I tried to figure out where to sit.

There wasn't much choice. Izzy had already taken the chair between the grown-ups and Vanessa, which would've been my first pick. It occurred to me that once upon a time, I could've just given Izzy a look, and she would've moved and let me have it.

The only seat left was between Shelby and Tori, all the way at the end. Shelby looked up, widened her eyes like somebody had just poked her, and turned her head toward Ginger, who was on the other side of her. They had a silent conversation I couldn't translate.

Tori saw me too, and she nodded toward the empty seat. She didn't smile, but she didn't scowl either. She didn't do anything, actually.

I inserted myself into the chair just as Sir Devon started talking. In his usual fancy way—it always sounded like his words must have had curlicues—he said he wanted input from each of the groups now that we had all read the script and had seen how we fit together. Then we could ask any questions we wanted to.

Tori's hand went up. "I just want us all to give a major 'Bravo!' to the writing group. The script rocks."

There were cheers all around while I tried not to stare at Tori. She'd always been the last one to speak up in class, like she wanted to stay under the radar so no one would look at her. I never even noticed her until one day last February when I saw how her eyebrows were getting ready to meet in the middle and told her they needed to be waxed.

I wasn't considering my smudges back then.

The conversation continued around me. The acting group said they had all the parts given out, and kids were learning their lines. Ginger said it was hard for some of the Latino kids, but they were working on it. I stared at her too. She didn't sound like a megaphone. And she didn't laugh like a hyena when Mitch high-fived her. She was almost normal. Not cool, but not, like, annoying.

The writing group asked for suggestions on the script, and next to me, Shelby wrote them down. When my eyes just kind of drifted down to see what she was writing, she edged the notebook away from me and guarded it with her hand.

Okay, *what*? What did she think I was going to do? Did she still think I was going to make her do stuff she didn't want to do? Could nobody just *forget*?

I think that's a trigger.

Ya think? On a shotgun.

Big breath. In and out.

"We haven't heard from the dance groups," Sir Devon said.

Vanessa took over, but I couldn't listen. Across the table, Ophelia brushed her lips with the end of her thick blonde braid, and I could tell she wasn't listening either. Twice she caught me watching her, and I looked away and then when I looked back, she was checking me out.

I think I might have pulled that trigger, except she didn't look the way Shelby was acting, all suspicious. She just seemed . . . curious. I guessed I couldn't blame her. I wasn't rolling my eyes or passing a note to Izzy or any of the things she probably expected me to do. And she couldn't hear what was going on inside my head—

"Kylie?"

I flipped my face toward the adult end of the table, where Mrs. Bernstein was pointing her chin at me.

"Did you want to report on our group?"

I just looked at her.

"The little ladies-in-waiting?" If she nodded her head anymore, she was going to get motion sickness.

"Um," I said. "Yeah, so, the Wee Dancers have learned the dance—"

"Wee Dancers?" Ginger said. "That's so cute! Oh, sorry!"

She clapped her hand over her mouth, and Shelby put her arm around her.

"It *is* cute, Ginge," Ophelia said.

If Shelby thought so, she wasn't saying. I was still wondering what had made me say that out loud.

Mrs. Bernstein nodded me on.

"Yeah, so, they're excited and, um, I did have one question."

"Perfect," Sir Devon said. "It's time to segue into questions."

I didn't know what that meant, but since nobody told me to stop, I said, "What about costumes? My—our girls are wanting tutus so bad they're, like, drooling."

"Ladies-in-waiting don't—" Ophelia started to say, until Tori nudged her. "I mean, do ladies-in-waiting wear tutus?"

"I have no idea," I said. "I'm not up on my castle wear."

The whole table laughed. I wasn't sure exactly what was so funny, but since nobody was looking at me like I'd just said something completely stupid, I decided it was okay.

"I could draw you some pictures," Ginger said.

Heads bobbed. People murmured that was a good idea.

"Wait," I said. "Who's doing the costumes?"

"Each group will be responsible for their own," Sir Devon said. "I've talked to the adult directors about that."

"We don't have to go all out," someone else said. "These kids' parents don't have a lot of money."

I felt myself sag. Felicity was going to be so disappointed. I batted away an image of her up there leaping with her tummy sticking out from under yet another faded T-shirt.

"I can totally help," Ophelia said to the whole group. "We have more costumes than we do regular clothes at our house."

I caught a glimpse of Izzy's face just then. She was practically suffocating so she wouldn't laugh. Translation: *Oh, do you* have *regular clothes? I've never seen you wear any.*

"Good meeting," Sir Devon said. "Is my production team satisfied?"

"Yo," Mitch said.

That must have meant yes.

"We're good," Tori said.

"Then we're adjourned. Go and eat hearty."

Something happened at the table. It was like all at once every-one around me let go of the energy they'd been holding back. Shelby shared her notes with Ginger. Ophelia waved her arms and announced all the periods of costumes she could pull out of a trunk. Tori leaned across the table trying to get Winnie's attention, which she couldn't do because Winnie was being high-fived by Mitch. Mitch was actually high-fiving everybody, and I decided to get out of there. Not because she might try to high-five me.

Because she might not.

Chapter Twelve

Finally, *finally*, I could talk to Lydia. On the way home, I wanted to go over all the things I had to tell her in my head, and I could totally have done that with Mom driving because she either didn't talk or she talked about stuff I didn't really have to listen to.

But Mom didn't pick me up that day. Dad did. In his black Corvette with the top down.

"Cool car!" I heard some kid say as I got in.

I wasn't sure why, but I wanted Dad to pull away quick before more kids saw us. Maybe it was Mr. Devon saying, *These kids' parents don't have a lot of money.*

"Surprised?" he asked as he took the curve out of the gate. Did boys always show off, no matter how old they got?

I grabbed the hair flapping in my face and nodded.

"Did you have lunch?"

"Sort of."

"You have room for ice cream with your daddy?"

"Now?" I said.

"Absolutely now."

"I can't."

His teeth flashed in the sun. "Why? You have a date? Let me at this guy—"

"I have a session with Lydia."

He mouthed her name like he was trying to remember who she was.

"So give her a call," he said.

"I can't."

Dad snapped his fingers. "I forgot your other surprise. Here—"

He reached into the console and pulled out my cell phone.

"You can have this back. Call her."

I started to reach for it, but I couldn't take it. It was like I was afraid of it—like maybe it had evil powers.

Okay . . . I'd been around that arts camp for too long.

But still I said, "No, Dad, I can't. Don't turn left here. I need to go home, please."

Dad pulled up to a red light and looked at me through his sunglasses. The lenses were so dark I couldn't tell if his eyes were smiling. Just because his mouth was didn't really mean anything.

"It's okay. I'll call her. We'll make other arrangements." He reached over and tapped my nose. "Come on—I don't have many chances to listen to my daughter. That's what you said you wanted, wasn't it? Lynda won't mind."

Lynda? Really?

I hadn't felt like I'd wanted to scream at somebody in a while, and I wasn't planning to start now. Deep breath.

"I'm going to have to disagree with you," I said. "Lydia *will* mind, and so will I. So could you please take me home?"

First, Dad looked like I'd just erased his brain. Then his face hardened with the smile still on it. Finally, he laughed, and it was even more fakey than the smile.

"I guess you've graduated from princess to queen," he said. "All right, your highness. I'll take you home."

That called for another *I have to disagree*, but I didn't feel like talking at all. Not when he just didn't get it.

∾

I was at the front door waiting for Lydia when she got there, and I barely let her get into her seat and pull out the tea thermos and the gnome mugs before I started talking. I told her about what happened at the movies and about the Instagram campaign and how I shredded my rules for the friends I no longer had and how I told Dad I wasn't a princess anymore.

It was all coming out mangled and confused, but Lydia took it in so calmly, just like she always did. But when I got to the part about the production meeting and how I felt like an alien sitting there with all those people who didn't just *like* one another—they *loved* one another—it was like something sprang up in her. She leaned so far out from her seat I thought she'd fall out and her eyes grabbed mine and held on.

"I want you to stop right there," she said, "and I want you to just be with that feeling for a minute."

No. It hurts.

"Stay with it, and tell me exactly what's going on."

It hurts!

"Try to tell me," Lydia said.

I had to swallow twice before I could say, "I don't belong. With the little girls I do, but I don't belong with anybody else."

"Name that feeling."

It hurts!

"It's bad. It's like being alone, only there are all these people around."

"It's lonely. What else?"

"That's all."

Lydia waited.

It hurts!

"Okay, and it's sad. I used to have friends like that, kind of, only not like they do."

"Why didn't you have it?"

"Because we weren't that kind of friends, I guess."

"Sounds disappointing."

It hurts!

"Okay, it hurts, all right? It hurts and I can hardly stand it. It hurts!"

I let my hands swallow up my face. But after only a second or two, Lydia pulled them away. Her tiny fingers were warm but soft and dry.

"I know it hurts, and I'm sorry," she said. "But you know what?"

"No."

"I think you can make yourself a new card."

A card? Now? Really?

Lydia nodded. I wasn't surprised anymore when she knew what I was thinking. I might as well just say it.

"Will a card make me stop feeling like my life is sliced up?"

"Not at first. Did you ever have your tonsils out or anything?"

"When I was seven." I fought off another wave of Missing Margaret. She was with me every minute of that whole tonsils thing, making me the best tea in the world and reading the entire Ramona Quimby series out loud at least three times and singing me to sleep with "White Coral Bells," a song nobody else I knew had ever heard of. It wouldn't have mattered. I wouldn't let them sing it to me if they did. Only Margaret. She left just a few months after that.

"Did we strike a nerve?" Lydia said.

"Kind of."

"After they cut out your tonsils—"

"Eww! Did you have to say it that way?"

"Actually I did, and here's why. They had to take out that part of you because it was constantly getting infected and making you sick."

And Mom was tired of me missing school and going to the doctor. Margaret said there were other ways besides surgery. They took that one and only argument I ever knew about out into the hall, but I heard enough to know Mom wasn't happy with Margaret "interfering." Mom told her to remember who was paying her. At seven years old, I didn't get it. I did now. In this exact minute.

"Right after the surgery, you were in pain, right?" Lydia went on.

"For a couple of days, until Margaret gave me some stuff she mixed up. Honey and something else."

Lydia's dark eyes sparkled, Felicity-style. "Did you get any infections after that?"

"No. I haven't been sick since."

She opened the thermos and filled the gnome cups. Suddenly, I couldn't wait to wrap my hands around one of them.

"When you talked about your life being sliced up and how much that hurts," Lydia said, "that reminded me of having surgery. It has to be done or you'll go on being sick. Right after it happens, you feel worse than you ever did before. But when the healing starts, you get why you had to go through pain to get well." She handed me a hot mug. "That's what's happening to you."

"Do you really think it's going to get better?" My throat was thick, and I didn't care.

"It's already getting better. Look at the progress you've made in the last week. And you've even discovered something I hadn't brought up yet."

Lydia pawed around in the red bag that seemed to have no bottom and pulled out a blank card and a purple marker. I sipped while she wrote, *Take Off Your Mask*, and pushed it toward me.

"Did I do that?" I said.

"You've done it several times. You told your dad you're not a princess." Lydia pretended to be pulling off something that was stuck to her face. "With the Winnie thing. You let go of having to be the only one everybody looks to for answers." She pulled off another imaginary mask. "You let a whole room full of people hear you call your girls the Wee Dancers, and they got to see your sweet side."

"Okay, I might be healing, but I don't think I have a 'sweet side.' I mean, really?"

Lydia laughed and pushed the mask card closer to me. "Add that to your collection," she said, "and let's watch it work."

"Do you want to see my other ones?" I sounded like Felicity wanting me to watch her dance in the parking lot. What was happening to me?

"O-kay," Lydia said.

For once, she didn't know what I was talking about. I opened my notebook and nudged the cards out of it. When I spread them on the table, her eyes danced. I know you read that in books, but hers actually did it. I think they were doing hip-hop.

"Kylie, I had no idea," Lydia said as she looked at the pictures I'd drawn on them. She cocked her head at me in a different way, like she really was surprised. "You are a girl of many talents. The more you become you, the more they're going to come out. It just works that way." Then she glanced into my empty mug. "More, my dear?"

"Please, Milady," I said.

∾

That afternoon Mom went out, although she didn't take her racket with her or her gym bag. Come to think of it, I hadn't seen her rush out to play tennis for about a month, not since the day she said nobody showed up. Jocelyn said she was going to lie out by the pool, and she invited me to join her. Mr. Hollingberry was working on the inside of my room, so we wouldn't have to compete with his power tools.

I smothered Jocelyn in sunscreen, and she smothered me. The whole time I was trying to decide whether to tell her about some of the stuff that was happening to me. That "fake it till you make it" thing wasn't working, but not pulling the trigger and considering my smudges and taking off my mask, maybe those were. She made the decision for me: soft little snores erupted through her lips before I even got the cap back on the sunscreen.

I never took naps. Not even when I was little, although Margaret always insisted on a "rest period." I'd thought about her enough for one day. Maybe I should work on my project out here.

Good idea. As I was passing through the kitchen to get my stuff, the phone on the wall rang. Who called on the landline anymore? For some reason I answered it.

"Kylie?" a familiar husky voice said. "It's Tori Taylor."

I would've known it anyway. The question was, what to do about it?

"I have something important you might want to know, so don't hang up."

But I did.

I was about to continue on to the stairs when the phone rang again. I let it go to voice mail, and I listened to her message the way I used to listen when Heidi or Izzy reported in with what people were saying about me: I didn't want to hear it, but I had to.

"This message is for Kylie . . . Kylie, you might want to ask your parents to do something about what's on Instagram today. We call this a Report Alert. Lydia taught us . . . well, anyway, that's all I wanted to say. I hope you get this."

"It is *way* too hot out there," Jocelyn said from somewhere. "I'm turning into a raisin." She opened the refrigerator. "Is there anything but diet stuff in here? What are you having?"

Through all of that, I stood staring at the phone on the wall. I felt like a snow cone with all the syrup being sucked out of it. I must have looked that way too because Jocelyn tossed her towel on the table and came to stand between me and the wall phone.

"What just happened?" she said. "I heard the voice mail—"

"Did you hear what she said?"

"Who? No, I just heard talking." She gave me a long, green squint. "Who was it, Kylie? You look like someone just slapped you."

When I didn't answer—because my tongue had turned to crushed ice—Jocelyn poked at the phone, and Tori's husky voice filled the kitchen again. It sounded so out of place, just like mine would be at her house.

"So we need to check Instagram," Jocelyn said. She was already going for her phone.

"No," I said. My tongue was starting to thaw. "She probably wants me to see it so I'll be humiliated."

"Who is this Tori person?" Jocelyn said.

Someone who never tries to humiliate anybody.

I still shook my head. "I'm not supposed to be on the Internet anyway."

Jocelyn tapped expertly at her phone screen. "No one's going to know."

Dad wouldn't care if he did know. He tried to give my cell phone back to me. The fact that Mom might not either made me shake my head one more time at Jocelyn.

"Will you just erase it? I'm going to go do my homework."

As I made my way up the steps, I heard Jocelyn say, "Who *are* you?"

Chapter Thirteen

The Fourth of July weekend was a way less fireworks and sparklers holiday than any I could remember. I used to be in the parade in Nevada City with my gymnastics school until I quit, and I was Little Miss Grass Valley one year and rode in a convertible with the mayor. Riannon's, Heidi's, and Shelby's families and mine always got together at Riannon's house for a party that lasted until the fireworks made their sparkly big blossoms in the sky. Not this year.

It was so hard to think about all that, so I stayed in my room and wrote up my social studies project. Kitty Margaret was afraid of fireworks anyway. I wanted to crawl under the bed with her and stay there until Monday.

I'm afraid nobody would even look for me.

I felt okay while I was awake. I couldn't do anything about what happened when I went to sleep. I hadn't had nightmares since I was five and went through a period where I was climbing into bed with Nanny Margaret every night. She said it was because I was starting kindergarten and everything was new. "Many adjustments, Wee One," she would tell me. "Your dreams are your fears making up stories while you sleep. So when you wake up, you can say, 'Things really aren't that bad.'"

It worked back then—along with graham crackers and milk in the middle of the night. But the dream images of me on Instagram with my face turning into The Chin Freak and Mr. Jett with a pointy head and then Osama Bin Laden and finally a zombie messed up my sleep. For three nights in a row, I sat straight up at three a.m. with sweat all over me like it had been sprayed on. Felicity had nothing on me.

Finally, Monday came, and I could be back with Milady and the Wee Dancers. This was the day when our group was scheduled to watch the actors do the scene with the ladies-in-waiting so they'd understand how their dance fit in. Once they got over their disappointment because the princess and her suitors weren't in costume, they sat like perfect ladies . . . okay, that's wrong. They sat behind the white line on the floor just like they were told to, but as soon as they got into it, they started the whole getting up on their knees thing and the stretching to get a little closer to the action thing, until Felicity and Pilar and Nicky were practically in the royal throne room.

I was just thinking that was pretty cute when Izzy gave this gigantic exasperated sigh and stuck out her foot. Before I even realized what she was about to do, she pulled it back and gave Felicity a shove with it.

Felicity burst into tears. Milady Bernstein gave Izzy a look that would have withered a house plant. Izzy left in a huff, and Felicity wailed that she had to go to the bathroom because snot was running into her mouth.

Other than that it went great.

I found a tissue for Felicity and sat with her on my lap for the rest of the scene. She leaned into me until I was sure I would have a perfect wet imprint of her on my brown T-shirt when we got up.

The scene the actors put on was actually good, and I had at least five ideas I wanted to run by Milady Bernstein before Tuesday's class. In a few days, it would be our turn to show our dance to the actors, and I wanted the Wee Dancers to make them go, *Are you serious? These kids are amazing!* Mostly, I wanted it for Felicity. She could live on that glow until she was ten.

She squirmed so much during the last two minutes of the scene I knew she really did have to use the restroom, so as soon as the clapping was over, I escorted her out of the rehearsal studio cabin. Ginger was at the door, talking to the girls as they burst out—in that same *Wow!* way they did about everything.

"Did you like it?" Ginger asked Felicity.

"I *loved* it!" Felicity said. "I can't wait to be a lady-in . . ." Felicity looked up at me.

"Lady-in-waiting," I said.

"Yeah, that."

"You'll be so good," Ginger said.

Felicity was by now doing the pee-pee dance, so I nudged her forward, but she wasn't done with Ginger.

"What are *you* gonna be in the play?" she asked.

"I'm helping the dragon learn how to be scary," Ginger said. And then she demonstrated, arms over her head, mouth and eyes open farther than I thought mouth and eyes *could* open, letting out a roar that . . . well, I was surprised it didn't come with flames.

Felicity squealed. If we didn't get to that bathroom within the next five seconds, we'd be looking for a change of clothes.

"Gotta go!" I said to Ginger and steered Felicity to the restroom building, which fortunately was a few yards away.

"Anybody else have to go potty?" I called out.

But the rest of the Wee Dancers were halfway back to our studio, bowing and curtsying to one another along the way.

"Go with them and get them started, would you, Kylie?" Milady said as she hurried out of the acting studio behind me. "I'll be along after I tell Izzy to bring Felicity back. She needs to apologize to her anyway."

Milady went one way, and the Wee Dancers were going the other. I stood in the middle, sort of stuck there. The Wee Dancers couldn't be left alone for more than about a minute before they'd be drawing with crayons on the mirrors or ending up in a puppy pile in the middle of the floor. But should Izzy be left alone with my Felicity?

My Felicity.

Besides that, would Izzy mean it if she said she was sorry? And if she didn't, wouldn't Felicity know it?

I leaned toward the dance studio. No out-of-control squealing yet. I looked back at the restroom. Milady was just coming out and heading my way. I ran in that direction.

"I need to use the bathroom myself," I said. "I'll be right back!"

"Can you give them a minute?" Milady said. "Izzy is still waiting for Felicity to come out of the stall."

"I'll wait outside first," I said.

Milady Bernstein started to hurry past me, and then she stopped, ponytail swaying, and touched me on the wrist. "It's nice working with you, Lady Kylie."

I mumbled a *thanks* through the thick stuff in my throat.

The restrooms were in their own little building with a porch outside, complete with railing and a bench, just like it was somebody's house. My plan was to listen at the window on the girls' side, and if Izzy's apology wasn't for real, I was going to . . . well, I hadn't gotten that far yet.

I was three feet from the steps when somebody behind me said, "Kylie? Could I talk to you for a minute?"

I had to turn around to see that it was Ginger. Since she stopped talking like one of those horns on a ship, I didn't always recognize her voice anymore. Matter of fact, she didn't even look the way she used to. It was like more red hair had been added to her head and less chubbiness hung out around her waist. It suddenly struck me that if Abigail was like me as a kid, Felicity was like Ginger.

Complete with the tiny beads of sweat on her upper lip, which shone there when I crossed the path and faced her around the corner of the rehearsal building.

"Did I really scare that little girl when I was doing my dragon?" she said.

"Felicity," I said.

Ginger nodded. "Did I? Because I didn't mean to."

I shook my head. "Felicity totally gets into things. She still thinks the Disney princesses are real."

"They're not?"

I blinked at Ginger, and she grinned, which made her very-blue eyes shiny.

"So I guess your dragon was pretty real to her," I said, "and she freaked out for a minute."

"You sure? Because she ran off to the bathroom."

"She had to pee. For real."

Ginger still looked doubtful. I couldn't really blame her for not believing something I said. While she was obviously deciding, I realized two things. I was having a conversation with the girl I used to call Gingerbread, like that was a disease. And she didn't look like she was even a little bit afraid of me.

"I'll still apologize to her," Ginger said. "But thanks."

"Whatever," I said.

The word *awkward* came to mind, but Ginger smiled and shrugged and bounced into the building all at the same time. I waited until she was gone before I rounded the corner and crept up onto the restroom porch to catch Izzy's apology. When I listened outside the window, though, I couldn't hear anything. And when I went inside, nobody was there. They must have come out when Ginger and I were talking.

That was the shortest "I'm sorry" on record. And from Motor Mouth? Jocelyn wouldn't believe it.

By the time I got back to the dance studio, it was lunchtime. I looked around for Felicity so we could walk to the dining hall together, but I didn't see her. I turned to Izzy, who was changing into flip-flops.

I said, "Where's—"

"Fatty Fee-Fee? She didn't just have to pee, she had to—well, okay, so it was diarrhea, and she needed to go home."

I didn't even know where to start.

"Did you, like, walk her to find Sir Devon?" I said.

"No. She didn't want me to. I watched until she got to the—"

"Where is Felicity?" Milady Bernstein said at Izzy's elbow.

I left Izzy to explain it all to her. For one thing, I wanted to find Felicity myself. And for another, I didn't want to be there if Izzy referred to her as "Fatty Fee-Fee" in front of Milady. That wouldn't be pretty. And I was tired of ugly.

Felicity was nowhere in sight in the dining room, and neither was Sir Devon. When I sat down at our table, Abigail said, "Where is *she*?" and pointed at Felicity's chair like she was accusing it of swallowing her up.

"She went home sick," I said.

Pilar's enormous brown eyes drooped at the corners. "She is sick?"

"She's faking it," Abigail said.

"What?" I said. "How would you even know that?"

"Because she was totally fine at the acting thing. She was all . . ." Abby demonstrated Felicity bouncing up and down. She actually had her down.

"I don't know," I said. "Maybe it just came on her all of a sudden."

"What if she doesn't come back?" Nicky said. "She won't get to be in the show."

All the heads bobbed, except Abigail's, and even she didn't say, *That's fine with me because she can't dance anyway.*

What she did say was, "Is she sick too?" and pointed to Izzy's chair.

"I hope so."

It was said in a voice so tiny I thought it was my own wee one. But it came from Daniella. I looked around the table with the words, *What am I going to do with this?* in my head, but from the way they were all suddenly going after the hot dogs that had just been put on the table, I figured they hadn't heard her. I wasn't even sure I had, so I leaned into her and whispered, "Why do you hope Izzy's sick?"

Daniella licked the pink lips that were already pretty wet. They were always wet. "Is she your friend?" she asked.

"I don't know," I said.

Her eyes—also always wet—grew bigger. "Sometimes she's not nice to us."

I glanced at the rest of the Wee Dancers, but they were currently taking turns making pictures on their buns with the mustard.

"Give me an example," I whispered to Daniella.

"She says if we don't try harder, we won't be better than your group, and we're trying as hard as we can, but she still says mean things."

"It's not polite to whisper at the table," Abigail said.

This from the kid who would tell you that you looked hideous in a tutu before she even knew your name.

"She's the teacher," Callie said. "She gets to do whatever she wants."

They all looked at me with their big innocent eyes like they were waiting for me to tell them the answer to, like, the question of the century.

"I had to talk to Daniella about something important," I said. "Could somebody please pass me the mustard? I want to make a picture too."

They got up on their knees in their chairs and leaned in and watched me draw a yellow frog on my bun and forgot about my whispers with Daniella.

But I didn't.

The worst part was that I couldn't talk to Lydia about it that afternoon because she was still out of town for the Fourth of July weekend.

No. The really worst part was that not long after Dad got home from work that night, when it was almost dark, he banged on the door of Jocelyn's suite and burst in with Mom right behind him before I could say, "Come in." Good thing Jocelyn wasn't there.

"Did you hear that message for you on the landline?" he said—without even saying hello or faking a smile.

I watched Margaret disappear under the bed. "What message?" I asked.

Mom darted out from behind Dad and stood next to him. They both had their hands on their hips. Not to be disrespectful, but they looked like Barbie and Ken.

"You know what message," Mom said. "From that Taylor girl."

"It's harassment," Dad said.

I *thought* I knew what that was—

"And I won't have my daughter harassed in her own home."

Wait. I wasn't the one in trouble here?

"Did you go on Instagram and look into what she said?"

"No, Dad," I said. "I'm not supposed to go on the Internet or any-thing, remember?"

"I don't think there's anything on there," Mom said. "I think she was just baiting you."

"I'm calling her father," Dad said.

My backbone stiffened from the bottom up. "No," I said. "Don't do that!"

"Don't even start with me, Kylie. I give in to you on everything else, but not this time. They've taken this too far, trying to draw you out and then pounce on you."

What was he even talking about? Whatever it was, it wasn't true, I knew that for sure. And if he started talking like this to Tori's father or Mrs. Yeats, I never *would* get back into school.

"Please don't, Dad," I said. "I don't like Tori that much, but she's not like that."

His eyebrows practically shot up to the ceiling. "Of course she's like that. She's the one who started all this in the first place!"

"No, she's not. I am!"

I was pretty sure even the ceiling fan stopped right then. They both stared hard at me. I couldn't blame them. I wanted to stare at me too.

But it was the truth.

Dad turned to Mom. "Are you checking in when that Lynda woman is here?"

"Lydia!"

They didn't look at me this time.

"What?" Mom said.

"She's clearly filling Kylie's head with all this . . . pscyho-babble."

"I can't be in there every second!"

"Well, we're done with her."

"No!" I said.

"We can't," Mom said. "This is the only way she's getting back into school."

"Forget that school. I'm this close to having her in Roseville."

"No!" I said again.

"So what happens if you don't get her in? Where are we then?"

"We hire private tutors and homeschool her."

"No!"

Finally, they heard me. Finally, they looked at me. But I could tell from their eyes that they didn't really see me.

When Dad did speak, his voice was danger-zone low. "I always let you have your way, Kylie, but it isn't happening—"

"Oh, for heaven's sake, stop, Zach," Mom said.

We both looked at her. Something had changed, like somebody had smacked her in the face. She looked dazed.

"We're so close to getting through this. Let's just let it go."

Dad eyebrows were out of control. "How is she going to learn—"

"Not from standing here discussing it like she isn't even here."

Whoa. *Another* surprise.

My mouth was probably still hanging open when Mom turned to me and said, "Did you answer Tori's message?"

"No."

"Good. Don't. You only have a few more weeks to go."

"That's it?" Dad said to her. "That's what you've got?"

Mom didn't answer. She just walked out of the room, and Dad followed her, still yelling stuff with her not yelling back. The room was left cold. I coaxed Margaret out from under the bed and held her and wished I had some tea. With Lydia.

Chapter Fourteen

I was still feeling like I was walking sideways when Jocelyn dropped me off at camp the next morning. Maybe that was why I immediately felt like something wrong and heavy was hanging in the air. That, and the fact that as I approached the Gathering Place, I saw two things at the same time.

Sir Devon talking to a woman by a bench not far from the entrance, and Izzy running toward me with that I-have-news-you-*have*-to-hear look smeared across her paper-plate face.

Sir Devon and the woman weren't sitting on the bench, and that wasn't the only thing that told me their conversation wasn't cozy. The woman, who had her hair plastered down with bobby pins and wore a too-big Disneyland T-shirt that looked like it had been washed a lot of times, was talking hard and fast to Sir Devon and poking her finger way too close to his chest.

Out of the corner of my eye, I saw Izzy getting closer and her cheeks getting redder. But I couldn't stop watching the lady yelling-without-yelling into Sir Devon's face. He looked really serious but not afraid. I would have been. The lady was scary.

"Kylie!" Izzy said in a whisper like she'd had a sore throat for a week.

I put up my hand to her, but she obviously didn't get the signal because words kept coming out of her mouth in hoarse little explosions.

"*You* are gonna be so *happy!*"

"Izzy, shhh!"

"No, seriously. It's about—"

It was all I could do not to put my hand over Izzy's mouth. The lady was starting to raise her voice at Sir Devon, and other kids on their way into the Gathering Place were either slowing down to hear or hurrying past so they wouldn't. I wasn't sure why I wanted to know what they were saying. Maybe because I was starting to like Mr. Devon and I didn't want anybody messing with him. Or maybe I just had a bad feeling and I wanted to be wrong.

"Are you even listening to me?" Izzy said.

"No," I said.

"What is *wrong* with you?"

I didn't answer because the lady was stomping away from Sir Devon with her car keys jangling angrily in her hand. Any minute she was going to walk within a foot of Izzy and me, and if we didn't move, she might plow over us. I grabbed Izzy's T-shirt sleeve and pulled her out of the way just as the woman looked over her shoulder and said, "I'm not bringing her back until that girl is gone."

"I'm looking into it," Sir Devon said.

"I mean *gone.*"

The dust she kicked up as she passed us poofed over my sandals. Sir Devon clapped his hands and said, "Time for the Gathering, artists!"

How could he be so calm and cheery after somebody just got all up in his face?

"I know what that was about," Izzy said.

I moved my gaze from Sir Devon back to her. She was like a round coffee cup about to brim over with whatever news she had.

"How do you know?" I said.

"Because I heard some teachers talking. A kid told her mom that somebody threatened to hurt her if she didn't keep a secret." Izzy jerked her head toward the parking lot where a lady was climbing into an old dented car that sat low to the ground.

"I bet that was the mom."

"But you don't know that for sure."

I started toward the Gathering Place. Izzy walked sideways next to me.

"I know this for sure: the person who threatened her kid was . . . are you ready for this?"

"Izzy—"

"Wait for it . . ."

"I don't even want—"

"*Gin*-ger!"

I stopped and Izzy had to do the grapevine to keep from tripping, but her face was still overflowing like that wasn't all.

It wasn't.

"Do you want to know who the kid was?"

"No. I don't."

"Yes, you do. It was . . . Felicity."

Izzy searched my face the way that dachshund of ours used to when she was waiting for a treat. What did she want from me—some kind of reward? For telling me my favorite Wee Dancer was involved in this thing that probably didn't even happen because Izzy was as big a liar as I ever was?

I wanted to throw up.

"I don't want to hear any more, Izzy."

"Why? You always—"

"I just don't, okay?"

I wanted to hurry off, but her face was changing so fast I couldn't even look away. It contorted from shocked to hurt to angry and landed on *Fine. You just wait.* I think the word for that was *smug.*

And I so didn't care.

Izzy didn't try to talk to me about it the rest of the morning. Actually, she didn't try to talk to me at all, and I was okay with that. She was probably right about one thing: Felicity might have been the one whose mom took her out of camp because she wasn't in class. Either that, or she really was sick the day before. Either way I was sort of homesick for her. Even Abby asked me why I was so "funky."

I had convinced myself Izzy was making up the part about Felicity and Ginger, until lunchtime. No giggling and apple-sharing and calling out a *Bravo!* for no apparent reason came from the assistant directors' table. And Ginger's chair was empty.

I tried not to stare over there because I didn't want them to think I was gloating. I really didn't feel like I'd scored a victory because Ginger was in trouble, which was what Izzy expected. The thing was that I didn't even believe it was true.

I mean, just yesterday she was about to cry because she was afraid she'd freaked Felicity out. Why would she threaten her about some secret? Maybe Ginger wasn't supposed to be practicing her dragon on the little kids? But that was no secret. I saw it, and so did our whole class.

Izzy might have actually known something about it. But I didn't want to hear it from her.

At least I got to see Lydia that afternoon because she was making up for not being there Monday. I paced by the front door until she arrived. I was afraid Dad might have fired her without telling me or Mom. When she came in, lugging that Mary Poppins bag, I almost hugged her.

Once we got settled at the table in the library with our gnome mugs in front of us, Lydia went over me with her flashy dark eyes and said, "You want to tell me what's going on?"

I didn't even pause. I told her the whole thing about my dad and mom, including the part where Dad said Lydia was filling my head with "psycho-babble" and that he wanted to fire her.

Lydia poured me a second cup of tea. "First of all," she said, "I'm extremely impressed with your self-control."

"I don't want to be sent off to boarding school or something. So what's second of all?"

"I'm sorry?"

"That was 'first of all.' What's 'second of all'?"

"Ah. Yes."

She set down the cup and pulled a card out of the bag. I didn't groan.

"You need a creative one-liner," she said as she wrote on the card in aqua marker. "Something you can say to the people who don't get that you're changing."

"I need an example."

"It can't be snarky. Not like, 'You totally don't get me, but that's not surprising. Since you're *clueless*.'"

I let out a laugh that was more like a spit. Lydia grinned her watermelon slice.

"And it shouldn't be condescending. Know-it-all."

"Like . . ."

"Like, 'I've worked on myself, and you haven't, so of course you wouldn't understand.'"

"So what *is* it supposed to sound like?"

"This is the one I used to use—"

"Wait. What? *You* used to need one?"

"Oh, yeah. When I was way younger, I was bullied a lot. I got called every single one of the seven dwarfs, when all I wanted to be was Snow White."

I swallowed down a big wad of guilt.

"Then I got help from a mentor when I was about twelve, your age. Once I got the hang of accepting who I was and loving myself because God loved me, things started to change. So much so that if I hadn't had that mentor, I might have become pretty obnoxious. Somebody who used to get away with calling me Dopey would try it, and I'd go, 'It's too bad you're still so immature. I guess you'll grow up someday.'"

"Did you actually say that to people?"

"That and worse. I made *so* many friends that way." Lydia gave me a blank look. "Not."

"Did you ever find a good comeback?"

"I did. I had to pray about it a lot, and it finally came to me. Whenever somebody would treat me like I was still the doormat everybody could wipe their feet on, I'd say, 'That actually doesn't work for me anymore.'"

I waited for more, but she just tested her tea and added more from the thermos.

"That's it?" I said.

"That's it."

"Did it work?"

"You mean, did people stop making fun of me and acting like I didn't have feelings because I was 'different'? Mostly. In time. Some people didn't, but I made enough friends and got involved in enough cool things that it didn't bother me anymore."

Lydia sipped the tea again and nodded at it like, *Good job.*

"Here's the deal," she said. "This is not about changing other people's behavior. It's about changing yours because you really can't alter the way other people act. They might behave differently toward you, but that's just because you've made it easier, among other things."

"I don't know what my one-liner could be," I said. "Too bad it can't be snarky because I do that really well."

Lydia's eyes smiled. "Yes, you do. And as long as you're not hurting anybody, you're actually pretty funny. You'll find yours, and when you do, you can write it on here." She slid the new card toward me. "Can't wait to see what you come up with for your drawing."

"Speaking of drawing," I said, "can I do some on my Bill of Rights for Friends?"

"You absolutely can. How's that coming along?"

"It's pretty much done."

"Good. Is it ready for field testing?"

"You mean like trying it out?"

"Yeah."

But I don't have a group of friends to try it out on!

"It doesn't have to be done with *your* friends," Lydia said. "Any group that hangs together or works with one another could work."

"Do I just walk up to a bunch of people and say, 'Hey, wanna try out my Bill of Rights?'"

"I don't doubt that you could pull that off, but no. Think of a group of six . . . girls . . . who you know—"

"My Wee Dancers! That's perfect!"

"It absolutely could be. Any ideas?"

The pad of paper and the gel pens came out, and we went to work. Well, actually I did. Lydia just asked me questions. The time went by so fast and we were so involved, I totally forgot to ask her if she knew anything about Ginger being in trouble. When I remembered it after she was gone, I was glad I hadn't. It just didn't feel right somehow.

What felt even less right was that Felicity might be out of the class forever. She would be so good at this Bill of Rights thing. I wanted to help her find a one-liner. I wanted her to just be there.

I got an idea for her that night while I was waiting up for Jocelyn to come home. I'd found a scary movie to watch, and I was fumbling around under the bed for Margaret so she could watch it with me when my hand landed on something else soft and furry. It was that cheerleader teddy bear Dad had gotten me when he was trying to make up with me. It was just about right for a six-year-old, and whether Felicity was sick or it was that other thing, she could probably use some cheering up. Maybe Milady Bernstein could get it to her.

The movie turned out to be too spooky even with Margaret in my lap, so I went into the hall closet where my DVDs and my other stuff were being stored while Mr. Hollingberry finished my room. I needed something lighter to watch. Like Disney maybe.

Who knew where my DVDs were? I had to open every plastic bin and dig under stuff and never did locate even one. But I found something else that made me say, "Oh, yeah, baby," right out loud. Inside a plastic bag were all six of the T-shirts Mom got for me during our week at Disneyland when I was nine, one for each day. I'd only worn them once, so they were like brand new, and they were just the right size for Felicity.

I took the bag of shirts to the suite, tucked the cheerleader bear inside with them, and tied the top with a hot pink shoelace with sparkles on it.

"What do you think, Margaret?" I asked in the wee voice.

She blinked three times and purred. Translation: *Very nice indeed, Wee One.*

∾

I wanted to get to camp early the next day to ask Milady Bernstein to keep the bag out of sight so the other girls wouldn't feel bad that they weren't getting presents and to get her permission to use my Bill of Rights with the Wee Dancers; it might help them work better as a team, especially after what Daniella told me about the way Izzy talked to her group.

Jocelyn was more of an oatmeal-head than usual, having to get up when it was practically still dark, but after going through the Starbucks drive-through, she was awake enough to say, "You're really into this, aren't you? Again, I ask: Who *are* you?"

I didn't answer because I didn't know. I was just going with it.

I wasn't the only one who arrived early. When I walked up over the little hill from the gate to the Gathering Place, I heard voices coming from outside the tiny cabin where Sir Devon had his office. I slipped behind a half-wall that separated the water fountain from the entrance to the Gathering Place to listen because I recognized both of those voices.

It was Felicity. And Izzy.

Once I was safely where they couldn't see me, I realized I couldn't tell what they were saying. I could *see* them, though, and it was mostly Izzy who was talking. Her round face was as hard as a glass plate and dotted red like she'd fallen into a bed of poison ivy. Her mouth was barely moving, but it didn't have to because the message came through her eyes. Cold and stony. Translation: *Don't mess with me, or you will be so sorry.*

I might have waited, maybe tried to sneak closer so I could find out what was going on, if Felicity's face hadn't collapsed. Enough already. I started out from behind the wall, but then things happened so quickly I couldn't move fast enough to stop it. Just as Felicity started to cry, Izzy grabbed her arm and brought her little face up close to her own. More words snapped, and Izzy let go and took off around the back of the office cabin.

I didn't know whether to take off after her or go to Felicity. The decision was made for me when Felicity saw me and hurled herself across the path. When she threw her arms around my waist, she almost knocked us both to the ground. I half-carried her to the nearest bench, where she buried her face in my T-shirt and sobbed.

"What did she say to you?" I said when her shoulders finally stopped shaking. "What did Izzy say?"

"Nothing," she said.

She sat up straight, and before I could stop her, she wiped her nose with the back of her arm. I found some napkins in the bottom of my Starbucks pastry bag and dabbed at the tears on her face. She gave me a watery smile, until I said, "I know she said something to you. What made you cry?"

The tears started again, along with the shaking of the head over and over until I realized that I was making her more hysterical than Izzy did.

"Here," I said, "I have something for you."

I dug the cheerleader teddy bear out of the T-shirt bag and tucked it under her chin. Sobs turned to squeals like someone had waved a magic wand.

"This is our secret," I said, "because I don't have a toy for everybody. We'll leave it with Milady until it's time to go home today."

Felicity nodded and giggled and hugged the bear to her chest, eyes closed. I would have giggled myself, if I wasn't so ready to rip off Izzy's lips. The longer we sat there, with Felicity thanking me and telling me I was the best friend in the whole world, the more I knew going after Izzy's lips wasn't my job. Something nudged at my mind, something Tori said in her voice message. *Report Alert*. Was that it? Did it mean I needed to tell Sir Devon what I saw? I had always hated the whole tattletale thing—since the tales were usually told on me— but this felt different somehow.

I didn't have a chance to talk to him during the Gathering, espe- cially with Felicity pasted to my side. When it was over, I wanted to take the cheerleader bear and the T-shirts to Milady Bernstein and tell her about my Bill of Rights idea before class started. Talking to Sir Devon could wait until lunch. I could keep an eye on Izzy until then so she couldn't do any more damage.

One thing I did know from the Gathering: Ginger wasn't there, and her friends didn't shout *Bravo!* one time. That "something heavy" was still hanging over the camp.

Milady Bernstein took the copy of the Bill of Rights idea so she could read it while I worked with the whole group. I expected Izzy to be all sulky about that, but she kept looking at me like she had a secret she sure wasn't going to tell *me*. I really wanted to pop her one.

The Wee Dancers worked hard—even Abby—especially after I showed them the picture Ginger drew and told them to imagine themselves in those lady-in-waiting skirts, flowing around them like scarves.

"Do we really get to wear costumes like that?" Nicky asked.

Abby's answer was a disdainful, "No. They cost too much money."

Little faces crumpled.

"I don't know," I said. "But we'll have something pretty, I prom- ise. For now, just pretend."

They did, and it was precious. Felicity didn't even seem to mind that it wasn't an imaginary tutu.

I couldn't wait for her to open her bag of T-shirts when she got home. I wouldn't be there, but I could imagine. In fact, that gave me an idea.

While they devoured graham crackers and lemonade outside during the break, I slipped back into the studio where Milady was getting ready for the second half of class.

"When you give Felicity the teddy bear back at the end of camp today," I said, "could you give her the bag of T-shirts separately and don't tell her who they're from?"

Milady looked startled, like I'd snuck up on her or something. "Won't she figure it out?"

I tried not to roll my eyes. "This is Felicity we're talking about. And even if she does, can you just tell her it was somebody who . . . I don't know . . ."

"Somebody who loves her?" Milady said.

I just nodded. My throat was doing that thick thing again. I couldn't even tell her about Izzy. Maybe I'd be better after lunch, and then I could talk to Mr. Devon. Or maybe there was somebody else I needed to talk to first.

"Kylie, you with me?"

I jerked my chin toward Milady, who was looking at me all curiously.

"I'm sorry?" I said.

"Your Bill of Rights plan," she said. "Did you come up with that yourself?"

"It's part of my social studies project," I said. "With Lydia."

She nodded, slowly bobbing her ponytail. "I like it. You can start it tomorrow. That gives you tonight to get prepared."

"Can I ask you a question?" I said.

"Of course."

"Is Felicity going to get to stay until the end of camp?"

Milady's eyes flitted like she wished I hadn't asked that question.

"For now," she said finally. "Mr. Devon is still working on that."

Okay. So I *did* need to talk to him.

"Can I ask *you* a question?" Milady said. "How did you know Felicity wasn't just sick yesterday?"

"Can I answer that later?" I asked.

"Yes," she said. "I trust you completely."

It was a good thing she didn't ask me to teach the second half of the class because I was way too choked up. Instead, she had me sit on the "throne" and be the princess for the girls to dance around, using some of the moves I'd taught them that morning. I didn't really like that role, even though I'd had a lot of practice.

I somehow got through lunch, which wasn't so hard because the girls were excited and talked nonstop all the way to the ice cream. And Izzy wasn't at the table, so that helped. She didn't show up until the dining hall was dismissed and I was heading for the assistant directors' table. Where she came from, I didn't know. Suddenly, she was just there, between me and the person I wanted to talk to.

"So are you never speaking to me again or what?" she said.

It was my turn to be startled. Izzy had never looked like she was annoyed with *me*, until now.

I couldn't answer because I didn't know. There was a lot of not-knowing happening for a girl who knew everything. I didn't plan on talking to Izzy about any of it, but now that she was here . . .

"I do have a question for you," I said.

"Wow," she said, eyes rolling until they disappeared. "What an honor."

"What were you talking to Felicity about this morning?"

The rolling eyes got wide. "When?"

"Early. Before the Gathering. You were getting onto her about something by Sir Devon's cabin."

"No, I wasn't." The eyes were darting now.

"I saw you," I said. "I was over by the water fountain. Why were you making her upset?"

There was much blinking before Izzy answered, "She was already crying when I found her there. Her mom was inside talking to Ponytail Man, and she was freaking out, so I was trying to get her to calm down."

"By grabbing her arm?"

"I thought she was going to run away."

"So why did *you* run away and leave her standing there hysterical?"

Izzy gave a huge frustrated-sounding sigh. "She was *fine*. I had to go do something for Mrs. Bernstein."

"What something?"

"You're not the *only* one she asks to do special things."

Izzy's attitude was back. But I knew she was lying. She was never quite as good at it as the rest of us. The only one worse was Shelby.

Speaking of which . . . I craned my neck to see around Izzy, but none of the other assistant directors were there. Including Tori, the one I wanted to see. I would've talked to any of them, including Shelby, to find out more about the Report Alert. But they were gone, and I realized after another gaze around the dining hall, so was Sir Devon.

"You still didn't answer my question," Izzy said. "Are you speaking to me or not? Because I'm not going to follow you around like a little puppy dog anymore, waiting for you to toss me a treat."

I almost laughed. "Where did you get that from?"

"From—"

I waited.

"I thought it up myself."

"Uh-*huh*."

"So *are* you?"

"I never asked you to follow me around like a little puppy dog."

"You expected me to."

I looked down at my toes peeking out of my sandals, showing off the last pedicure Jocelyn treated me to. Pieces of the pink polish had chipped off, and I hadn't even noticed.

"I'm glad you're not doing that anymore," I said to Izzy.

When I looked at her, she was backing up. A soft collision with a chair stopped her. "I'm just going to say you wouldn't tell me straight out," she said.

"Say to who?" I said.

Her eyes went totally wild, and she crashed away through the dining hall, leaving tablecloths lopsided and napkins knocked to the floor. She was clearly on a mission of some kind, trying to find out if I would talk to her. Three guesses who sent her.

And I didn't care about that either.

My path through the tables was slower than hers, so when I got outside, there was hardly anybody left in camp. Except Tori.

She was hanging out on the same bench I'd seen Sir Devon and the mad mother standing by. She had her feet up so she could face Sir Devon's office cabin, and she was staring at it as if she were going to throw herself at it the second the door opened.

I went straight to her and stood looking down at her.

"Can I ask you something?" I said.

She pulled her feet off the bench and patted it for me to sit next to her. That felt weird, but I did it. She lifted her lanyard and fiddled with it. The whole thing must have felt weird to her too.

"What's a Report Alert?" I said.

She let the lanyard drop. "You listened to my message."

"Yeah. You said me telling my parents about the Instagram thing was like a Report Alert. What is that?"

"You haven't told them yet?" Tori's brow was all puckered.

"They heard it," I said. "But I'm not talking about that. It's about another thing."

"What other thing?"

She was way more . . . concerned . . . about this than I expected. Maybe I still thought she'd be suspicious of me.

"We're against all kinds of bullying," she said. "No matter who it's happening to."

"So you'd be against it if it was happening to one of the campers. The little kids."

"Well, ye-ah."

I knew she almost said, "Duh!"

"So if I even think I know somebody's being bullied, but I'm not sure, should I do one of those Report Alert things?"

Tori nodded. The sun seemed to like her hair somehow. "You would just say you suspected something so the grown-up could keep an eye on it."

"Is that what you're going to do?"

"Huh?"

"When you go in to see Sir Devon?"

Her shoulders sagged. "No. I wish I did know something. I just need to . . . . talk to him."

"Is it about Ginger?"

That was when the suspicion shield fell down over her face, so hard I could almost hear it.

"It's personal," she said.

"Do you know why Ginger isn't here?" I said. "Is it because Felicity's mom accused her of threatening Felicity? Because I don't think it was Ginger. I think it was . . . somebody else."

Tori looked like she was writing a five-paragraph essay in her head. It was hard, but I waited till she was done.

"I can't talk about Ginger," she said—at last. "But if you know something that could help her, you should definitely tell Sir Devon. That's a Report Alert."

Then I was right. And it was the first time in my life I really didn't want to be. Izzy might be a lying, sneaking, mean little . . . person. But she used to kind of be my friend.

And yet there was Felicity.

"Okay," I said. "Do you care if I wait here too?"

Tori shook her head just as a horn blew at the entrance to the parking lot. It was Mom, waving her arm for me to hurry.

"Let's get ice cream," she called to me.

I had to go. But before I left, I looked back at Tori. I hoped she translated that as: *I'll try to do the right thing.*

Mom and I didn't talk about much over sundaes at the Lazy Dog. She acted like chocolate syrup was poison, and I didn't know whether to ask her if Dad was "letting it go" or not. She did try to get me to chat about school clothes and how I wanted my room decorated, and I guess I answered. Mostly, all I could think about was Felicity and Ginger and Izzy and Sir Devon. I wished it was a Lydia day.

Chapter Fifteen

Thursday morning, though, I was ready for camp, Lydia or not. Ginger still wasn't there at the Gathering, and I still didn't get to talk to Sir Devon. Felicity slipped in late and clung to me like a koala bear. She was wearing my Little Mermaid T-shirt, and I had a hard time not saying, "Do you like it? I wore it at Disneyland!" I was disappointed that she didn't tell me about the whole bag. The only thing she seemed interested in was never being more than an inch away from me. It was kind of like being in a three-legged race.

I managed to get her to sit in the half circle in class next to Pilar, and I wished she had her bear with her to hug. She just seemed so afraid, and she kept glancing at the door.

As for Izzy, she sat behind the girls and texted.

I shook off all of that and sat down cross-legged, facing the Wee Dancers.

"We're going to learn something that's not exactly about dancing this morning," I said. "But it's going to help you dance better together."

"I don't get it," Abby said, tossing her blonde curls and hitting Nicky in the face with them.

"You don't have to be nervous," I said, "because I'm going to explain it all to you."

My eyes met Abby's, and she bit her lip. Translation: *You really get me, don't you?*

"First, we're going to learn a new rule. I've put it on a big card for you."

I picked up the half piece of poster board that I'd put facedown beside me on the floor and turned it toward them. They got up on their knees and stretched out their little necks to see. A few of them mouthed the words, and Nicky read out loud, "I will listen to my dancer friends and not interrupt."

"I like the big ears you drew on the girl," Felicity said.

Yes. She was participating.

"You drew that?" Callie said. "It's so—"

"I do listen," Abby burst out, "but I don't get how this has anything to do with our dance."

I pressed my lips together, so I wouldn't smile.

"I think you just gave us a good example, Abby," Milady said. I could tell she was trying not to smile too.

"Come up here, Ab," I said, standing and holding out my hand to her.

Lucky for me she skipped up to join me.

"And . . . Nicky, you come too."

I stood them facing each other. I whispered in Nicky's ear and then said to Abby, "Will you please show Nicky how to do that one part where you curtsy to the princess? She's having a little trouble with that."

Abby hesitated for, like, a nanosecond. "Okay, so you first stand like this . . . and then you bend this leg and then you . . ."

I tugged Nicky's sleeve. Except for the giggle, she was right on cue. "That doesn't make sense," she said. Loud and strong, like she'd been waiting to say that to Abby since birth.

Abby stopped, put her hands on her hips, and said, "You have to listen and follow directions."

Nicky looked at me, and I gave her a high-five.

"What?" Abby's voice was curling up way high. She'd be screaming in a minute.

"It doesn't feel good to be interrupted by your friend when you're showing her something, right?"

"Right," she said.

"So . . . wouldn't Nicky learn a lot faster if she didn't get all up in your face and interrupt you?"

"Yeah. Du-uh."

I squatted down so I could look Abby in the eyes. "Then don't do it," I said.

And then, for some reason, I hugged her. She was kind of like a statue in my arms, but at least she didn't pull away and go, "Eww, gross! You touched me!"

Milady and I put them into three pairs and had them teach each other the curtsy, promising to listen and try what her partner said. Izzy was still texting, so I had to work with two groups. Milady seemed to be heading for Izzy, hand already out to take away the phone, when the door banged open and a woman came in like a storm ripping through the room.

"I'm taking my daughter home!" she said.

It took me a second to realize she was the same lady who was talking to Sir Devon, with the bobby pins and the angry face.

"I sorry. Mrs. Lane, is it?" Milday said.

She had switched her path from Izzy to the woman, who was just about to plow through the pairs of Wee Dancers. I pulled Felicity and Pilar behind me and held out my arms. Felicity was already crying.

"I'm taking Felicity home!" Mrs. Lane said. "Where is she?"

Izzy snapped a picture of her. Milady snatched the phone from her. I pushed Felicity's face against my back.

"Mrs. Lane," Milady said, "I think we should both go speak with Mr. Devon—"

"I already told him I'm taking my kid home until that girl gets some kind of punishment for threatening her."

She looked around the room like a wild woman, and Milady nodded at me.

No! Protect Felicity!

I wanted to listen to my wee voice, but slowly I turned so I could get Felicity in front of me and still hold her against me. She was sobbing her little heart out.

"Did you see the bruises on her arms this morning?" Felicity's mom asked.

Felicity tried to pull her left arm up into the too-big sleeve of the *Little Mermaid* shirt, but her mom grabbed her hand and shoved up the sleeve. The whole room gasped. On Felicity's upper arm were four black-and-blue places shaped exactly like fingers.

Something flashed through my mind.

"And yet you let that girl come back. I saw her going into Mr. Devon's office when I got here." She put her hand behind Felicity's head and shoved her into her side. If that was a hug, it was a pretty rough one. "So either that girl goes or my Felicity goes. And—" She rifled through the contents of the bag on her other shoulder. "Don't think teddy bears and T-shirts are going to buy me off."

She pulled out the teddy bear cheerleader.

Felicity cried out and tried to grab it, but her mother threw it in Milady's direction, and it plumped against the wall and fell to the floor.

"My bear!" Felicity said.

I took a step. I was going to get that bear and I was going to—

But Milady said, "Kylie, will you please stay here with the girls while I walk Felicity and her mom out?"

I wanted to say no. I wanted to say I could prove who did it and it wasn't Ginger.

But the five Wee Dancers who were left were all looking at me, eyes filling up and little hands all fretty and distressed. I couldn't leave them. Not with Izzy.

Who was currently following Milady, trying to get the cell phone she had taken hostage.

When all four of them were out the door, I gathered the Wee Dancers into their semicircle and tried to smile.

"See what happens when somebody interrupts?" I said. "It gets everybody upset. C'mon. Show me how you can curtsy."

We curtsied until lunchtime. I figured the Queen of England herself would be impressed.

Izzy wasn't at lunch. Neither was Sir Devon. Or Felicity. Or Milady.

But Ginger was.

She was sitting at the assistant directors' table in her usual chair, but nothing else was "as usual" in the group. Ophelia had her arm around Ginger, whose face was as pale as Winnie's. Tori was talking to the group, and everybody was nodding to her, except Shelby. She was tearing up a napkin. She always did that when she was nervous. When she sat at my table at Gold Country Middle, the napkin-shredding went on a lot.

Maybe I was wrong. They were tighter than my posse had ever

been, and maybe it wouldn't work to go over there. How was I going to prove what I knew anyway?

And then Ginger did something that changed my mind again. While Tori was still talking to her, she spread her fingers across her face, like she was pressing back the tears. Freckled fingers. Wide fingers.

The empty chair was still there, and I had to go sit in it. But then, there were the Wee Dancers, who were just now getting back to giggling and finding creative things to do with their food. Should I leave them?

"Do you mind if I join you ladies today?"

I looked up to see Milady slipping into Felicity's chair beside me. "Yay!"

"Could you sit by me?"

"No, me! Oh, wait—I interrupted."

"I'm going to take that as a yes," Milady said.

I took it as a go.

"I'll be right back," I said to her.

And before I could find any other excuses not to, I went straight to the empty chair at the assistant directors' table and said—I guess because it was fresh in my mind—"Do you mind if I join you ladies today? For a minute?"

Shelby clearly minded. She grabbed another napkin. Everybody else nodded. They didn't say "Yay!" and "Sit by me!" But they nodded.

Weird and strange and awkward as it felt, I went right to what I came for.

"I think I can help prove that Ginger didn't threaten Felicity and grab her by the arm. I can do a Report Alert. If you want me to."

"We don't need your help," Shelby muttered. I only heard her because I was expecting it.

Mitch nudged her, and she went back to making confetti.

Tori looked around the table before she said, "Ginger is being bullied by somebody—"

"So of course we considered the usual suspects," Ophelia said.

She could have used my "friends don't interrupt" card.

Winnie whimpered, and Tori gave Ophelia a look I was sure she could translate.

But I said, "I know that means Izzy and me. I get that. I even get that when I swear to you I didn't have anything to do with it, you probably still won't believe me."

Mitch poked Shelby.

"But I was talking to Ginger when that whole threatening thing supposedly went down. So she couldn't have done it."

All eyes went to Ginger, who went from Winnie-pale to Felicity-red in zero-point-two seconds.

"I had to make sure that little Felicity girl wasn't freaked out when I was doing my dragon thing!" Ginger said.

"It's cool, Ginge," Tori said. "Nobody ever said you couldn't talk to Kylie."

"Yeah," Mitch said, "so why didn't you tell us?"

"Or Sir Devon?" Ophelia said.

Ginger stared at the tabletop. "Because I just didn't think . . ."

"You just didn't think these guys would want me involved," I said. "I get that too. I guess I wouldn't trust me either. But seriously, I can help."

"I'm sorry," Shelby said. "But you *can't* trust her."

"So one of you go with me. Ginger. Or Tori." I had to swallow. "Or both."

Nobody said anything. I scraped my chair back.

"Okay," I said. "There's one part of this that doesn't affect you guys, and I'll just tell Sir Devon about that."

"You should," Tori said. "Just like I told you yesterday."

I couldn't help wondering what the rest of her group said to her about *that* after I left the table.

When I got to Sir Devon's office cabin, loud voices came through the tiny window, and I knew one of the voices belonged to Felicity's mom. The other one was a man's, and it was kind of familiar, but it wasn't Sir Devon's.

I knew I should probably wait, but I was done with that. I knocked on the door, and when everybody got quiet, I went in.

At least, I tried to get in. The office was barely big enough for two people, and there were four crammed in there already: Sir Devon, Felicity, her mom . . . and Mr. Hollingberry.

I made five. Well, maybe still four, since Felicity was under my arm before I could get the door closed behind me. We were like one person.

"Sorry, Sir Devon," I said. "But I have something to tell you."

"I'm tired of hearing this," Felicity's mother said.

But Sir Devon's sort-of-gray, sort-of-blue eyes looked tired too and he said, "Please, Mrs. Lane. I'm just trying to compile information here. Kylie, what can you tell us?"

He beckoned for me to join him at the front of his desk, which was shoved against the wall, probably to make room for all these bodies. Mrs. Lane had taken the only chair, and Ginger's dad stood behind her. He was so tall he sort of had to hold his head to the side so it wouldn't hit the ceiling. It seemed like anger wanted to come out through his freckles.

Mrs. Lane pulled Felicity into her lap, and I leaned against the desk beside Sir Devon. My toes almost touched hers.

It was time to tell them what I realized when I watched Ginger pushing back her tears with her hands.

"If you look at Ginger's fingers," I said. "And you look at the bruises on Felicity's arm, you'll see that the marks don't match." I glanced up at Mr. Hollingberry. "This is not, like, a put-down, but Ginger's fingers are way bigger."

"You a friend of hers?" Mrs. Lane said to me.

"No," I said, "I'm not. I just think she shouldn't be accused of something she didn't do."

I felt Sir Devon sigh beside me. "Would you like me to bring Ginger in?" he asked.

Where would we put her?

But Felicity's mother said yes, and Mr. Hollingberry went to get Ginger. While we waited, my heart tried to pound out of my chest. What if this didn't work? What if Ginger's fingers weren't as big as I thought they were? That whole group was going to think I was just trying to humiliate her. Again.

When she and Mr. Hollingberry crowbarred their way into the room, I realized I'd never seen them together before. They looked a lot alike. And he was holding her hand so that her freckles danced to meet his.

Please, please, please let this work.

Yes.

"You explained this to Ginger?" Sir Devon said to Ginger's dad.

He nodded.

"Ginger, would you mind?"

Ginger shook her head and maneuvered past her dad and around the chair with the Lanes in it. The whole time she didn't take her really-blue eyes off of me. I was glad when she got there, so I could squish myself against the wall and not have to look back. It didn't occur to me until then why I had trouble making eye contact with Ginger. It made me feel so guilty.

"Felicity, may I see your bruised arm again?" Sir Devon said.

Felicity bobbed her head. "She's the dragon lady!"

"What?" her mom said.

"Ginger's teaching the dragon how to be scary," I said. "For the production."

That didn't seem to help Mrs. Lane, but Felicity smiled a teary smile at Ginger and held out her arm. I still wanted to gasp at those bruises.

"Ginger, would you try to match your fingers to these marks?" Sir Devon said.

"Gently," Mrs. Lane said.

Really, lady?

Ginger looked at the bruises for a few seconds and then tried to arrange her fingers just above them. Felicity's mom looked almost disappointed when she shook her head.

"They don't match."

"Of course they don't," Mr. Hollingberry said. "Because she didn't do it."

Sir Devon looked at Mrs. Lane and said, "May I?"

"Do whatever," she said.

Sir Devon picked up Felicity and set her on the edge of the desk. Ginger retreated to her dad. I watched as they held hands again.

"Felicity," Sir Devon said in a voice so kind it made me want to cry, "when we asked you who was threatening you, telling you bad things would happen if you told her secret, why did you tell us it was Ginger?"

Felicity looked suddenly frozen.

"Have you ever seen Ginger before?" he said.

"Who's Ginger?"

"That's Ginger right there," Sir Devon said, pointing.

NANCY RUE

"That's the dragon lady."

Sir Devon tucked in his chin. "I'm confused, Felicity. Help me figure this out."

I *already* had it figured out.

Tell them!

"You said Ginger was saying mean things to you. But that's Ginger right there, and you say she's *not* the one who said those things."

Felicity shook her head. I had seen her look pretty miserable before, but this topped all other times.

"Then why did you give us the name *Ginger*?"

"Because—"

"Because why?"

"Because she'll—"

"Who?"

"She'll tell Lady Kylie I hate her—and I don't! I love her!"

Felicity came off the desk and into my hug. I squeezed her tight so I wouldn't cry.

I just couldn't cry now.

"Who is 'she'?" Mrs. Lane said. Her voice was shrill, like Felicity was the one who was in trouble.

Felicity shook her head against my shirt.

"Lissy, you tell me!"

"I know," I said.

Eyes pointed at me like daggers.

"What are you saying, Kylie?" Sir Devon said.

"I'm saying I know who probably told Felicity to say that."

"Who is it?" Mrs. Lane said. Now *I* was the one in trouble. Could this woman never speak like she wasn't a cop?

I got Felicity unstuck from the front of my shirt and put my hands on the sides of her face so she couldn't look away.

"It's okay to say who it was who told you to lie."

"She'll hurt me again!"

"She can't. But you need to tell us."

"Okay. It was Izzy." Felicity twisted to look at Ginger. "I'm sorry I got you in trouble."

"It's okay," Ginger said. "I understand."

Nobody in the room could doubt that she did. Her face was so sweet; I wished she understood *me* too.

"So this Izzy person will be taken out of here?" Mrs. Lane was saying to Sir Devon.

"It will certainly be handled," he said.

"Felicity won't be back until it is."

"I want to come back tomorrow!" Felicity cried. "I want to be in the play and wear a costume and be with Kylie!"

"Not if I can't be sure you're going to be safe!" her mother cried right back at her.

Sir Devon looked at me and nodded toward the door. I knew he wanted me to leave, but . . . what if this lady wouldn't listen to him?

A second nod sent me out the door. Mr. Hollingberry and Ginger were right behind me.

"Thank you, Kylie," she said. Her eyes were shiny again. "And I'm not even mad at you for saying I had fat fingers."

"I didn't say that! I just knew they were bigger than Izzy's."

Mr. Hollingberry caught my slip-up right away. I could see it in his startled blue eyes. Ginger was probably still too happy about not being kicked out of camp to notice that I knew, really knew, it was Izzy all along, even before Felicity confessed.

Ugh. Izzy.

"I need to go take care of something," I said and ran for the studio. My stuff was there, plus Izzy might be. I was pretty sure she hadn't gotten back her phone from Milady, and she definitely wasn't going home without it.

I was right. Izzy was sitting outside the studio with her bag, arms folded, sort of staring at nothing. Or at least that was how it looked until she saw me. Then her eyes went into slits. I wondered for a second if she had any facial expressions she didn't learn from me.

"Now are you speaking to me?" she said.

"Oh, yeah," I said. "I am *so* speaking to you. Why did you tell Felicity to say Ginger threatened her? Why would you *do* that?"

She didn't even blink. "At first, I did it to show you that I'm not just a little puppy dog. I can do things on my own."

"What 'things'?"

"Getting rid of them, one by one."

"Who?"

"Tori and all of them. Riannon and Heidi use me. You use me. So I thought I'd prove that I could do just as good by myself. It's like—"

"Izzy, that doesn't make any *sense.* We can't be doing stuff like that or we don't get back into cheerleading."

I stopped. Wow. That sounded like the lamest thing that could come out of somebody's mouth.

"What?" Izzy said.

"Nothing," I said.

"Well, then, when Ginger got in trouble and you didn't get what I was doing, I thought, *Too bad for you, Kylie.* So I decided to get back at you."

"By telling Felicity you would tell me she hated me?"

"Sheesh, did that little brat tell you *everything*?"

"First of all, she's not a little brat. And second of all, she not only told me, she told Sir Devon and her mother and Ginger and Ginger's father."

The color in Izzy's face drained out, but she didn't back down. "So? It's her word against mine."

"And against mine."

Izzy shook her head.

"Oh, yes, Izzy," I said. "If you don't go turn yourself in to Sir Devon and tell him you're a different person than the way you acted, I'll tell him what I saw."

"You're threatening *me* now?"

"No. That's just the way it is. 'Cause if you don't take responsibility, then I have to take responsibility."

"You *want* me to get in trouble—now that you have everybody thinking you're all goody-goody?"

"I'm trying to keep you out of bigger trouble than you're already in. I'm telling you, Izzy, it's way better to admit you messed up. Then you can change the way you act."

"So I'll be like you? I don't want to be like you anymore, Kylie. I used to, but I don't now. Heidi and Riannon are right. And you just wait. You're gonna be so sorry."

I was already sorry. Sorry for her. Because Sir Devon was headed down the path, straight toward us. Milady was behind him, and they both had bad news all over their faces.

"I hate you, Kylie," Izzy said.

A sound came from somewhere, or maybe it was inside me. It was like a big metal door clanging shut. Closing down on the last friendship I had.

I went inside the studio for my bag. When I came out, they were all gone. Suddenly I was empty—

Not empty. Free.

Chapter Sixteen

I couldn't wait to tell Lydia that afternoon. I was, in fact, about to zip open like a bag stuffed too full. I even told Mom that on the way home. Sort of.

"I have a lot to talk to Lydia about today," I said. "So could we not make any stops on the way home?"

Mom didn't say anything for a minute. I was about to repeat myself when she said, "She isn't coming today."

I felt like antennae were rising out of the top of my head. "Why not? Did Daddy fire her? He didn't, did he?"

"No, I talked him out of that." Mom pulled up to a stoplight and squeezed the steering wheel.

"Is something wrong with Lydia?" I said. "No—she was fine Tuesday. She's okay, right?"

"You really like this woman, don't you?"

I didn't even think about it. I just said, "Yes. Please tell me what's going on."

Mom turned, heading away from our house. "Lydia thought it

would be a good idea for you and me to have a session today, by ourselves. So I thought a table outside at the Briar Patch? It's not too busy at this time of day on a weekday—"

"You and me?" I was breaking my own rules, but I did not get this.

"She and I have been meeting once a week," Mom said.

"To talk about me?"

"No. To talk about me and how I can be a better mother."

"Oh," I said. That was the last thing I'd expected to hear.

"We had coffee that one time so she could tell me what she planned to do with you, and she suggested that maybe I wasn't modeling the best behavior for you."

I could imagine Lydia saying that. I just couldn't imagine Mom putting up with it.

"It ticked me off at first, but a couple of other things happened..."

I wanted to break in with, *Like what?* but I held myself back this time.

"I called her and asked if we could meet, and we've been doing it ever since."

Mom nosed the car up the hill leading to the Briar Patch, the natural food store where they had the best little individual pizzas in the whole entire world, as far as I was concerned. But I couldn't even think about food.

"So, what are we supposed to talk about?" I said.

"I think I'm going to do most of the talking today," Mom said. "I want to tell you what I've learned."

That was exactly what happened after we got our pizzas and smoothies with all kinds of weird stuff in them. I was too blown away to say much anyway. Here's what she told me that day. I'm leaving out all my interruptions because, um, there weren't any.

She said when she was my age she was "Miss Popularity," and she had been really proud when I got that role in middle school. But she never told me that because she was really busy with entertaining and her friends and playing tennis and keeping up with everything. Because she wanted to be, well, *Mrs.* Popularity.

She said Jocelyn was right when she said she spent more time with me than Mom did. And when she tried to hang out with me, she realized she didn't even know how to talk to me.

And Mom said she didn't get why everybody was so upset about the whole "bullying" thing—not until she was telling Heidi's mother, after she and Riannon's and Shelby's mothers didn't show up to play tennis—that she had done that stuff when she was a kid, and it was no big deal. Heidi's mom told her she *still* acted that way.

I remembered her talking on the phone with me listening around the corner. That must have been the conversation because she didn't play tennis after that.

She told me that Lydia helped her see that she and Dad weren't giving me consequences for the things I did wrong. And that even taking away my phone and my Internet was just to appease Mrs. Yeats, not to teach me anything. She said Lydia showed her that they didn't make me take responsibility for my choices—they let me quit dance and gymnastics when things didn't go my way—and they blamed everything on Ginger's and Tori's parents "overreacting."

"But they weren't," Mom said, with actual tears in her eyes. "If someone bullied you like that, I'd be up at that school so fast."

I thought about the Instagram thing and Tori's warning on her voice mail. I *was* being bullied. Should I tell her what that was about?

Mom set aside the pizza plate, with the slice she hadn't even touched still on it, and looked at me. I was uncomfortable because . . . this was new. It was like she was interested. In me.

"Lydia says you have really turned around and that she wouldn't be surprised if you became a leader in the anti-bullying thing, right alongside that Taylor girl."

"Tori," I said. I didn't add that I wasn't even close to being the leader Tori was. Huh. And to think I was once determined to take her down for depriving me of everything. Everything I didn't want anymore.

"I'm proud of you, Kylie," Mom said. "I really am."

I shook my head. "Don't be. I'm not that good."

She tossed back her hair. "Then I guess I'd better show you that you are."

I used to wonder why it took Ginger so long to tell her dad we were harassing her. Now I knew. She was ashamed of being bullied. And so was I. Izzy practically told me it was still going on. I almost knew how not to be a bully anymore. But I didn't know how not to be a victim.

∾

The next day at camp, Ginger was back for real—I could tell that from the many *bravos*, like their group was making up for the ones they didn't shout while she was gone. But Izzy wasn't there.

I raced to the studio ahead of the Wee Dancers to get to Milady.

"Morning, Lady Kylie!" she said.

"Did Izzy get kicked out?" I said.

"You always were one to get right to the point," she said, with an almost-grin. "No. We came down here to talk to her, and she didn't even give us a chance to ask her any questions. She just quit."

"Oh," I said.

Milady tilted her head. "You look a little disappointed."

"I was kind of hoping she'd do something different," I said.

"Like . . ."

"Like take responsibility."

Milady shook her head. There was no ponytail to sway today. She had her dark hair pinned up in a ballerina bun. "Izzy's not where you are yet. Should I say this?" She must have decided she could. "She wasn't much help, anyway. Most of the time she just took pictures, which apparently she was posting on Instagram when I took her phone yesterday."

I stopped breathing.

"The whole time you were talking to the girls she was back there at it," Milady went on. "She should have been listening. She could learn some things from you."

Unfortunately, she already had.

The next day, Saturday, Jocelyn and I planned to go shopping for school clothes. She was taking the chipped polish off my toenails because she said they looked "ratty" when there was a soft tap on the door. We both waited for it to open, but when it didn't, Jocelyn said, sort of impatiently, "Well, come *in*."

It was Mom.

"You girls going shopping?" she asked.

"That was the plan," Jocelyn said. "Kylie, be still. I don't want to get this on the bedspread."

"Would you mind if I went along?"

Jocelyn dropped the cotton ball, soaked in remover, and ran into the bathroom.

"What brought this on?" she called from there.

But I nodded at Mom. "Sure," I said. "Come with."

Mom looked like I told her she didn't have cancer or something.

"I'm ready when you are," she said. "We can look for things for your room too."

She smiled at me, looking a little nervous, I thought. I smiled back and she left. Jocelyn came out of the bathroom with a wet wash-cloth and scrubbed the bedspread like it had personally offended her. If the nail polish remover didn't take out the color, she was about to.

"All of a sudden she wants to be a mother," she muttered, more to the spread than to me.

"Lydia's been helping her," I said.

"Wonder how long that's going to last." Jocelyn looked up at me. "Sorry. I hope it does last because I won't be here for you."

"Me too," I said.

Jocelyn went back to scrubbing. "Well, at least there's one thing: she'll spend more money than we would."

I suddenly didn't care if Mom bought me anything at all.

∽

At least I didn't care until we were passing Champs at the Arden Fair Mall and there was the Jacket in the window. The one I wanted so badly back in June. The one that could still make me feel like I was already out on a football field on one of those brisk fall days, ready to cheer the seventh grade team on like nobody ever had before.

When I'd told Izzy we couldn't be bullying people if we ever wanted to cheer again, it seemed so lame. Maybe because it wasn't the real reason I didn't want to see Felicity or Ginger or any of her friends hurt. But I still wanted it. I still wanted to wear that jacket.

"It's not a done deal yet," Mom said at my side.

I jumped a little because I thought she'd gone to get us Cokes.

"But as soon as you're back on the squad, I promise you we will come back and buy it. And whatever else you want from this store.

Tennis shoes, definitely. You've grown so much this summer, I'm sure you've gone up at least a half size."

I nodded and we moved on—to Macy's and American Eagle, and Bed Bath & Beyond. Jocelyn got enough clothes to outfit her entire dorm. I wasn't that excited about anything else but the Jacket.

But as we started toward Ruby Tuesday for lunch, that's when I saw what I wanted . . . really wanted.

It—or I should say *they*—were in the window of Delilah's Dance Shop, swirling on mannequins of little girls, scarf-like skirts and ballerina tops and tall-coned hats with scarves of their own, in pink and blue and the mintiest of greens.

The perfect costumes for ladies-in-waiting.

"Mom!" I said. "That's what we need!"

"I'm not following," she said. At least she didn't say, *What in the world* for?

"For the Wee Dancers, for our production," I said. "We don't have costumes for them yet, and these would be so perfect. Please?"

"How many would you need?" she said.

"Six."

"Are you serious?"

"Yes," I said.

I got between her and the window so I could really look at her—and so she could really see my face.

"I don't need that jacket, even if I do get back on the squad. I don't need anything from Champs we couldn't get at Walmart." I thought she might faint, but I went on. "I'd rather have these instead."

"And what would you do with them after the production?"

"Let the girls keep them."

"I just really want to know what happened to my little sister," Jocelyn said.

Mom looked at her. "What do you think?"

"What do *I* think?" Jocelyn was half-laughing, but she looked like she was about to lose her balance just standing there. "I think . . . you should do what makes Kylie happy. 'Cause this may be the first I've seen her that way in a long time."

Mom's eyes got all teary the way they did at the Briar Patch, and finally, *finally*, she nodded.

"Let's go in and see if they have enough. Do you know the sizes you need?"

"Oh, yeah," I said and almost skipped into the store before I caught myself. I hadn't lost *that* much of my cool.

We came out with six of the best lady-in-waiting costumes ever. Ever. And I already knew how I was going to handle it on Monday.

Chapter Seventeen

M om got me to camp early like she was as excited as I was. She even wrote the note for the bag.

No one was in the studio yet, so I left the bag outside the door and ran for the Gathering Place. Some other people were showing up, so I sort of mixed myself in with them so nobody would realize I'd gotten there ahead of time. But one person did.

"Kylie," a husky voice said close to my ear. "Can we talk to you?"

I looked at Tori, searching those little bird eyes for what I might have done wrong, but she looked all concerned again, so I nodded and followed her out by the water fountain wall where Ophelia, Winnie, Ginger, and Mitch were waiting. Shelby wasn't with them.

"You helped us—well, helped Ginger—" Tori said.

"And that helped us," Ophelia said.

Yeah. She definitely needed my Don't Interrupt card.

"So we want you to let us help you."

Tori looked around at the group. They all bobbed their heads.

Mitch grunted. That must be Mitch for *yes* and just about every-thing else.

"Help me with what?" I said.

Tori nodded at Winnie, who pulled a cell phone out of her pocket. I didn't have Winnie figured for a phone type. In fact, I had never seen any of them with a cell.

"Shelby wouldn't come," Winnie said, her pale face turning pink from the inside. "But she let us use her phone to show you."

"Show me what?" I said.

Winnie turned the phone around. It was already glowing with a picture of me, sitting cross-legged on the floor of the studio, only my face was distorted so I looked like a witch performing a spell.

Winnie had to fumble to get to the next picture, which was me demonstrating a curtsy, except that the pose made me look like I was, um, going to the bathroom. I can't even repeat the caption.

When she swiped her finger on the screen to get to the next one, I said, "Okay. That's enough."

But Tori said, "There's one more you really need to see. Not because we want your feelings hurt, but because—"

"It'll show you that you really need to do a Report Alert," Ophelia said.

I was shaking my head, but Winnie got to the next picture, and Mitch took the phone from her and put it closer to my face. There was me, hugging Felicity—but my face was totally smirky and the caption read, *I hate these kids. The things I have to do just to be a cheerleader again.*

"No!" I said. "That's not true!"

"We know it's not." Tori tucked her hair behind her ears. "But this has to be stopped or all the good things you've done this summer will be totally ruined."

"And it's not fair." Winnie was obviously about to cry, and even though it had always seemed to me that Winnie cried over just about everything, I was still surprised.

It made my throat so thick I had trouble saying, "Who's going to believe me? All the grown-ups will think I haven't changed after all."

"In the first place," Mitch said, "my dad says you can totally trace this stuff back to the person who did it."

"You told your *dad*?" I said.

"I didn't use names or anything," Mitch said. With a grunt.

"See, that's how we do this." Ophelia's arms waved like lady-in-waiting scarves. "We gather information and then make a plan. It's how Lydia taught us."

I felt myself start to panic. "You haven't told her!"

"No," Tori said. "It's not our story to tell. We're just trying to help you tell it."

"Besides," Ophelia said, "you have witnesses that will say you never looked like that with Felicity or any other time at camp."

"Who?" I said.

Tori looked around at the group again, and they all said, at the same time, "Us."

I must have looked stunned because on the inside it felt like everything turned white. I couldn't even see them for a few seconds.

"Are you okay?" Winnie asked.

"Why would you do that for me?" I said. "All I ever did was try to make your lives miserable."

"You did a really good job too," Ginger said. "But I forgave you."

"No way," I said. "I never even said I was sorry."

"You didn't have to." Ginger smiled this kind of . . . wise . . . smile. "But I'm glad you know now."

What I didn't know was how that worked. I wasn't sure I could ever forgive Heidi or Riannon. Or Izzy. She hadn't been putting together a camp experience album. She was giving them ammunition for their Instagram campaign and all the time acting like she was still my friend.

"We think you should go to Mrs. Yeats," Ophelia said. "That's what we would do. And we'll go with you."

"But first you should tell your parents," Tori said. "I mean, if you can. If you think they'll understand."

"My mom might," I said, talking to myself more than to them. "But this feels like tattling. I'm used to handling things on my own."

"And ya see where that got ya," Mitch said.

I almost grunted *for* her because she was right. I just didn't want Mom and Dad storming into the principal's office, Mom demanding stuff and Dad going all Counselor for the Defense.

"Oh, and about tattling," Tori said. "A, tattling is when you tell to get somebody *in* trouble. B, reporting is to get somebody out of trouble. In this case, you."

"Will it ever stop, though?" I said. "If they get in trouble over this, won't they just retaliate, like they're already doing?"

"Not if you know how to stand up to it," Ginger said. "Lydia could help you with that."

"Wouldn't it be great if Kylie could work with her?" Winnie actually clapped.

I could only stand there, mouth open. Lydia hadn't told them we were already working together? But at least . . .

"I know who to tell," I said.

"Let us know if you need witnesses," Ophelia said. "We love to testify on somebody's behalf."

There was a time I would have laughed in her Drama Queen face. Now I said, "Thanks, you guys. Really."

Then I went to the bathroom instead of the Gathering so I could make myself not cry.

When I got to the studio, Milady had the Wee Dancers in their semicircle, and she was reading the note to them out loud. The bag was already open, so she'd apparently looked inside already.

"These costumes are for the most beautiful ladies-in-waiting in the kingdom," she read. "You will wear them to dance before the princess on your special night."

By then they were already up on their knees, necks like rubber as they strained to see. I sat behind them and pretended to be curious too. Sometimes the pretending skill still came in handy.

When the first costume came out of the bag, a pink one the color of strawberry ice cream, the squeals and oohs and little girl gasps filled the room like a choir of excitement. With each new one, the sound was more wonderful. But the most beautiful was Felicity crying out when the last one appeared: "There are six of them! One for each of us!"

It wasn't so much the sound as the fact that she was there at all. I wanted to shout, "The blue one is for you! It will match your eyes!' But, as Tori would put it: A, only a blue one was in her size, and B, she was never going to know I was the one who brought them. Nobody was.

Okay, so Milady looked at me with her eyebrows raised, but I just kept pretending I was as surprised as anybody. She didn't say anything about it after that.

The next step was handing them out and trying them on. Mom had written at the bottom of the note that there should be one to fit every "lady." It didn't take Milady long to sort that out, and she told the Wee Dancers they could put them on for one run-through of the dance, and then we would put them away and save them for the dress rehearsal.

All went well until Abby looked at Nicky, who had the pink version in the same size as Abby's green one, and said, "Give me that one. Pink is my favorite color."

Nicky didn't hand it over immediately—so at least she'd learned something—but after a moment of Abby giving her what could only be called "the stink eye," Nicky held out the pink dress.

I swooped in.

"I'll help you change into your green one, Abigail," I said, and half-carried her off to the bathroom building, costume and all.

She didn't scream along the way like I expected her to, and when we got inside, she just said, with her lip out, "I need that pink one."

"Why?" I said.

"Because it's prettier." Her little voice was quivery.

"Says who?"

"Me?"

"Why?"

"It just is."

The stubbornness was coming back into Abby's eyes, and I knew if we went too far into that, I'd never get her out.

"I'm just thinking there's another reason," I said.

She shrugged.

"I hardly ever see you wearing pink, but Nicky wears pink a lot. Isn't it *her* favorite color?"

"I guess so."

"She looks pretty in it, doesn't she?"

"I guess so."

I wanted a *yes*, but I went on because Abby was looking at her toes and talking in a voice like a mouse.

"Are you afraid Nicky will look prettier than you?"

No answer. That was better than a *no*!

"Here's the thing, Ab," I said. "Nobody's prettier than anybody else. You're all going to look pretty. It's about how you dance, not about the costume—that's what makes you beautiful."

"What if I don't like green?"

"Why don't you decide that after you put it on?" I asked.

I waited by the sinks while she went into a stall, and I looked in the mirror. I looked in the one at home every morning when I did my hair and stuff, but this kind of looking was different. *I* was different. My face seemed smooth or maybe relaxed? Was that it? Whatever it was, I knew one thing: I liked this girl. And I wasn't sure I had liked her since she was eight years old.

"Here I am," Abby said.

I turned around, and I didn't even have to try to smile. She was adorable, like an elf who slipped in for the dance.

"Want to see yourself?" I said.

I got down so she could use my thigh for a stepstool, like we did in cheerleading. I didn't have to ask if she liked what she saw. She said "Oh!" and I knew.

The other Wee Dancers were ready when we got back to the studio. They all curtsied for us when we came in the door, and they glowed like little fireflies. But no one glowed brighter than Felicity. She never could have rocked a tutu, but she did wonders for that scarf skirt.

∾

I wasn't planning to tell Lydia about the costumes that afternoon—although Mom made me tell *her* five times in the car, and it was very cool. I think I did tell Lydia because I wanted to put off reporting to her about the Instagram horribleness. I guess I was really procrastinating big time, since I also filled her in on the thing with Abby and the costume, and I didn't plan to do that either. It kind of felt like bragging.

Evidently, Lydia didn't see it that way. "You realize what you did there, don't you?" she asked.

"Kept her from pitching a fit?" I said.

"You rid the world of a potential bully—and you probably saved Abby from a lifetime of unhappiness. Or at least you took her a step in that direction."

I looked down at my fingernails. Up at the ticking clock. Over at the books lined up on the shelves that probably nobody ever read. Everywhere but at Lydia.

Of course she read my mind anyway.

"What else is up, my friend?" she asked.

If she had called me anything else, I might have just kept putting it off. But because she called me *friend*, I burst out with, "I need to do a Report Alert, and I don't know how!"

It was the first time I ever really saw Lydia look, well, astonished. Sheesh, I was sounding like Ophelia.

"A Report Alert," she said.

"Yeah. Tori and them taught me about it."

"I see."

"It's a long story—and by the way, why didn't you ever tell them I was working with you?"

Lydia shrugged. "It wasn't my story to tell."

It seemed like everybody was speaking the same language all of a sudden.

"And your healing is nobody's business but yours and mine and whomever else you want to share it with."

"It was like they already knew it was happening."

Lydia smiled the slice smile. "That's the best way. Now, about that Report Alert?"

"Something's happening . . . to me . . . and they think I should tell my parents, but I wanted to tell you first, just . . . because."

"Tell away, then."

I opened my mouth to do it. Really, I did. But nothing would come out. How to tell this person who thought of me as her friend that my former friends would do to me what I had done to so many other people?

"It's hard to admit you've been bullied, isn't it?" Lydia said.

"Okay, that's it," I said. "How do you always know what I'm thinking?"

"Because I've been there." She put her face closer to mine. "And because I don't want you to stay there. It's also God, I think."

"God?"

"I pray for you before every session and ask God to let me help you. He hasn't failed us yet."

"Even though I don't pray?"

Lydia put her hand on top of mine for the smallest of seconds. "Especially because you don't. And I'm open to that any time you want." She took away her hand and folded it with her other one. And waited.

I didn't let her wait long. "I guess I just feel like I deserve what Ri—what these people did to me."

"No one deserves it."

"Even if—"

"No one deserves it. If that were the case, bullying would just go on and on and on, and it doesn't have to and it shouldn't." Lydia leaned into the table. "You have a chance to do something to stop it, just like you did with little Abby. And I can't think of anybody stronger than you, Kylie. You've always known you have a powerful effect on people. Now you can use it for good."

I let that sink in. Really deep. Then I said, "Do you want to know what they're doing? So you can tell me if it's bad enough for a Report Alert?"

"Does it feel bad?"

"It feels horrible."

"Then it's bad enough. You can tell me if you want to. That's up to you."

I didn't think I could.

"I think I'll just tell my mom," I said.

"Good choice."

"Not my dad."

She didn't say anything. But I could tell from the way she tightened her hands that she thought that was an even better choice.

"Will you be praying for me when I do it?" I said.

"I'll be praying for both of you."

"I think I want to go do it now."

"I like that idea," she said.

So I found Mom sitting out by the pool, drinking an iced tea and reading a book. *A book?* I'd think about that later.

She did have her cell phone with her, so without saying anything, I got on Instagram and found the pictures. Then I turned it around and said, "I want you to see what's going on, and then I need you to help me figure out what to do because I don't know."

I held my breath while she flipped through the pictures and her eyes at first got wider and then narrower and narrower until they almost disappeared. I let out all the air when she looked at me and said, "This is unconscionable, Kylie."

I had no idea what that meant, but tears leaked from the corners of the eyes that were in tiny dashes just a minute before. She was sad for me. That was all I needed to know.

"I don't want to tell Dad," I said. "He'll just get all yelly and want Heidi and Riannon thrown in jail."

"You're sure it's them?" Mom said.

"Yeah. And Mitch's dad said there's a way to prove it is."

"Who on earth is Mitch?"

"She's a girl who's had experience with this. She and her friends are the ones who told me this was still happening."

"This is what the Tay—what Tori left the message about."

"Yes."

"Why didn't you—" Mom stopped herself, like she was tripping over her own next thought.

"Is Lydia still here?" she said instead.

"I think so."

"Let's go see her because I'm not too good at this yet."

As I followed her to the library, I heard her mutter, "What I really want to do is . . ." I didn't get the rest. That was probably a good thing.

Lydia helped us sort it out. Mom told her what was happening, although I wouldn't let her show Lydia any of the pictures. We decided Mom would call Mrs. Yeats and tell her what was happening. She probably wouldn't do anything about it because it didn't happen at school, but at least she would know I wasn't actually doing any of the things it showed me doing in the pictures.

"Tori and Ginger and everybody said they would testify on my behalf," I said.

Mom looked at me like I was speaking French.

"I'm sure those were Ophelia's words," Lydia said.

"They were," I said. "You know *all* of us pretty well, don't you?"

"I'm totally lost," Mom said.

Chapter Eighteen

It was hard for me not to push Mom to call Mrs. Yeats right that very minute. She said she wanted to think about what she wanted to say, and Lydia said that was a good idea. I was afraid she wanted to talk to Dad about it too, and he was out of town for a week. If I had to wait that long, I might go nuts from the fear.

What if Mrs. Yeats saw the pictures before Mom got to her?

What if Heidi and Riannon made sure she did?

What if Izzy made a prank call and said she should?

Yeah, I was going a little crazy.

But I had a lot of other things to distract me.

First there was the camp production, which was coming up in two weeks. Dress rehearsals started in just one. Our whole class decided not to tell anyone else at camp about the costumes. We wanted to surprise them at first dress. How those about-to-explode-like-water-balloons little girls were going to keep that a secret, I had no idea. But it was fun watching them try. Nothing better than a secret to bond girls together. Well, a good secret, that is.

I continued with the Bill of Rights every day. The Wee Dancers learned *You Are Not the Boss of Any Other Dancer and No Other Dancer Is the Boss of You. If Someone Is Mean to You, Tell a Grown-up.* And, of course, *We Are All Beautiful Just the Same.*

When the day came for Milady to decide who should lead the dancers in for the dance, she chose Abby, who was the most confident. And what did Abby do?

She looked around and said, "Does somebody else want to do it more than me?"

Whether they were all too shocked by the question or they really did know she was the best choice—who knew?—nobody said a word, and Abby proudly took her place at the head of the line.

Milady and I looked at each other, and we smiled.

Lydia and I only had a few more sessions left. She was going on vacation starting the Friday before the production, so she wouldn't be there. She said Mr. Devon was recording it, but I was still disappointed.

On the Monday before the first dress rehearsal, Mom came into the library to join us. Lydia must have known she was coming because she pulled three gnome mugs out of her bag and a bigger-than-usual thermos of tea.

"These are . . . interesting," Mom said.

"Don't laugh at my relatives," Lydia said.

I think what came out of my mouth was a guffaw. You know, a really big laugh. Mom didn't laugh that hard, but she did smile at Lydia. I guess she wasn't used to having friends who joked around with her either. Mom and I had a lot to learn together.

But right then, I had to ask, "What's going on? Why are we all here?" I zeroed in on Mom. "You talked to Mrs. Yeats, didn't you?"

"I only got to see her today because she's been out of town."

She could have *told* me that, but I didn't want to interrupt when she was on a roll.

"I showed her the Instagram pictures, and she was as horrified as the rest of us. And Kylie—" Mom shook her head at me, shivering her hair against her cheeks. "She never thought for a moment that any of it was true."

She looked at Lydia and said something about them being right, that nothing could be done by the school because it didn't happen there, during the school year. I didn't really listen. I was still back on what she said about Mrs. Yeats . . .

"You okay, Kylie?" Lydia said.

"She really didn't?" I asked.

"Didn't what?" Mom said.

"Think it was true?"

"How could she?" Lydia shook her head. "I've been giving her great reports about you all summer. And so has Mrs. Bernstein. And Mr. Devon."

"Besides," Mom said. "Their photoshopping was *very* sloppy. Clearly a fake. The woman is not stupid."

"So it's over?" I asked.

"Well," Lydia took a sip of her tea and gave it a nod of approval, "this does mean they have no reason to retaliate, so it will probably fade away."

"I still hate to see them get away with it, though," Mom said.

"Me too," Lydia said. "But in my experience, these things usually make their way to the surface, and often at the right time, if we wait."

Mom looked at me. "What do you say, Kylie?"

"I say we wait."

We toasted to that with our mugs, and I actually felt almost happy. But it was still hard to believe it was *over* over.

I knew Riannon and Heidi and Izzy better than anyone. Because I used to be them.

∽

Still, it was difficult *not* to be happy when dress rehearsal week came.

The rest of the camp gave the biggest *Bravo!* of the whole summer when our ladies-in-waiting came across the stage in their costumes. We actually had to have them enter again because the cheering was so loud they couldn't hear the music to do the dance.

Sir Devon was sitting next to Milady and me to watch and he said to her, "Where *did* you get those costumes? They are perfection."

"An anonymous donor," she said.

I decided that was the best thing I had ever been.

But then there was the Bowing of the Assistant Directors.

Sir Devon had this idea that he wanted all of us to take a bow at the end because we'd worked so hard to help the kids, and naturally, he wanted it to be a big deal. We couldn't just come out on the stage and drop into a curtsy or something.

He was probably right. It would be what my mom would call "tacky" after such an amazing production.

What I didn't think was particularly smart of him was putting me in charge of making it happen with the other assistant directors—meaning Tori and everybody. Really? He knew our history, right?

I didn't tell him he was a nut job, though. We just met like he said to on Tuesday during the second half of class time, onstage in the Gathering Place. Me, Tori, Ginger, Ophelia, Mitch, and Shelby. My first question: "Where's Vanessa?" I planned to give her the job, since she was the only eighth grader and probably thought she should be in charge anyway.

"She quit two weeks ago," Ophelia said.

Tori laughed. "You're not that observant, are you, Kylie?"

It felt like all the people were holding their breath, but I laughed too.

"Why'd she quit?"

"She got sick of doing stuff for other people," Tori said. "I'm not talking bad about her. That's what she told me."

"Oh," I said. "That's kind of the best part."

Shelby turned her back and took a couple of steps away from the group. I felt myself frown, but Winnie said, really quickly, "So what should we do, Kylie?"

"Do you guys have any ideas?" I asked.

Ophelia raised a long arm. "I think we should do a little skit, but I bet that's a bad idea, right?"

"It's an idea," Tori said.

"Okay, withdrawn," Ophelia said.

I had to stare for a minute because I'd never actually seen anything like that happen.

"What about something cheerleadery?" Ginger said.

Mitch gave a grunt that was definitely not a yes. I had to agree with her. I couldn't see her doing a stag leap, and if I recalled from gym class, Winnie and Ginger weren't the most coordinated. We were different sizes and shapes and usually cheerleaders were all alike. Only one thing would work and even that . . .

But they were all waiting for me to come up with something, so I said, "We could try a pyramid."

Shelby turned back around. "With you standing on top of course."

"Of course," Tori said. "She's the smallest and she's the most experienced—"

"I think it sounds fabulous!" Ophelia said, arms whipping around. "I've always wanted to do that."

"I don't know if I can." Winnie's pale brow was already puckering.

"It's really not that hard if you distribute the weight right," I said.

"I'd be on the bottom," Mitch said.

Whew. That saved me having to point that out.

Tori pulled a piece of paper and a pencil out of the pocket of her cargo shorts. Who carried stuff like that around with them?

"I think I can figure it out scientifically," she said.

She figured for, like, ten seconds, and she had it.

Mitch, Tori, Shelby, and Ophelia on the bottom. Winnie and Ginger on the next level. Me on top.

"Winnie *could* do the top," I said, only because I could feel Shelby glaring at me.

"No, she couldn't!" they all said in unison, including Winnie herself.

Shelby was still glaring. I had to say something or I was going to have a hole drilled into the side of my face.

"I'm totally open to other ideas," I said, looking at her.

"It's fine," she said.

It so wasn't, but at least I tried.

I taught them how to set up the pyramid out on the grass where nobody could get hurt, and it was pretty hilarious at first. Twice we ended up in a puppy pile. Once we almost had it, and then Ginger sneezed, and I jumped ship before the whole thing could collapse. Finally, we did it, and even though I had no idea what it looked like, it felt okay.

"This is going to be über-fabulous," Ophelia said as the bell clanged for lunch. Her braid was half falling out, and the rest of her hair frizzed out in a halo around her red face, but she and the rest of them looked like they'd just been to an awesome party.

Except for Shelby, who stomped off. Tori followed her and tried to talk to her, but she flounced herself away.

She wasn't at the assistant directors' table that day. Tori invited me to come, but I wanted to eat with the Wee Dancers. This was my last week with them, and that was our table.

Huh. I'd found it after all.

The next day, Wednesday, when we met to practice again, we were one short.

"Is Shelby in the bathroom or something?" I asked.

Everybody looked everywhere but at me. Winnie actually whimpered. There was no grunt from Mitch.

"It's me, isn't it?" I said.

Tori shook her head. "It's her. She's got trust issues."

"With me."

Nobody answered.

"Whatever," I said. "But we can't really do the pyramid with just six people." I didn't say *these* six people, even though it was true.

Ophelia folded her arms, which couldn't have been easy to do, long as they were. "I just don't see why she has to ruin it. You don't see Tori pulling this, and she really has a reason—"

"You have any another ideas?" Tori asked me.

For once I was glad to see somebody break the don't-interrupt rule.

"There's one formation I know that we can do with six," I said. "It's different, but we can do it." I looked at Tori. "You still have that piece of paper in your pocket?

I had Tori draw a star, and then we put people at the points. Mitch would be in the center on hands and knees. Tori and Ophelia would stand out to either side of her with one foot on Mitch and the other one the ground. Each would reach up a hand to me to pull me up onto Mitch's back. They'd keep holding onto my hands, and their other hands would be out to the sides. Ginger and Winnie would sit in front with one leg tucked in and the other leg spread out.

Yeah, Ginger and Winnie were so relieved I thought they were going to pass out.

It was actually easier than the other pyramid, but by the time we got it down, everybody's hands were sweaty, and they were losing their grips on me and each other as they got into the formation.

"I think I have some gymnastics chalk at home," I said. "It's more for, like, the parallel bars or whatever, but it'll help."

"It'll be just like the Olympics!" Winnie's voice was chirpy. I was almost starting to like it.

Thursday we had what I agreed (with Ophelia) was a "fabulous" time practicing the pyramid and deciding how to do our hair so it wouldn't get in the way and what we should wear with our brown T-shirts—because nobody wanted to use anything different. We decided on khaki shorts.

I knew Tori tried to get Shelby to come back. She even asked me if there was a place for her in our new formation, and I said yes because I knew Shelby did a great split and we could use that in front between Ginger and Winnie. It would be *so* cool.

But Shelby wasn't having it. I talked to Lydia about it on Thursday. She said some wounds take a long time to heal, but if I just kept doing what I was doing, either Shelby would come around or she wouldn't. It was her journey now.

Oh, yeah. I didn't control people's journeys anymore. Or anything else about them, for that matter.

"I hate that you're not going to be there for the production," I said, hugging my hands around my warm gnome mug.

"I'll be praying for you," Lydia said.

I looked into the milky tea. "Margaret used to pray over me."

"Margaret?"

I nodded. "She was my nanny until I was eight, and Mom and Dad sent her back to England. Every night when I went to bed or I was hurt or sick, she'd whisper prayers."

"Do you remember what they sounded like?" Lydia's voice was soft.

"It was like, 'Lord, bless my Wee One. Make her strong.'" I swallowed hard. "Like that."

"That must be why you've taken so well to what we've done all summer. You've had God in your life for a long time, and you didn't even know it." Lydia's voice got even softer, like a silk pillow. "I bet Margaret's still praying for you."

"I never got to hear from her again," I said. "Mom and Dad wouldn't let me talk to her because I got so upset."

"And that's where it began."

"What?"

"The hiding of the hurt."

I didn't ask her what that meant. Because I knew.

"I have something for you," Lydia said, "since this is our last meeting for a while."

If she hadn't reached into the red Mary Poppins bag, I would have been really disappointed. She pulled out my social studies project and slid it across the table to me.

There was a big blue *A+* on the front.

"This is beautiful," Lydia said. "It should satisfy Mr. Jett, *and* I'm recommending to Mrs. Yeats that she readmit you to school. Cheerleading will be up to Mrs. Bernstein, although—"

She didn't get to finish because I was out of my chair and around the table and hugging her before she could. The interruption rule didn't *always* apply.

Chapter Nineteen

Friday was the first time we assistant directors did our bow at dress rehearsal. It brought down the house, or it would have if we hadn't been outside. Afterward, though, Sir Devon came to us with worried eyes.

"That is astounding, ladies," he said to us. "But I have two concerns."

"One," Tori said. She really did talk like a little scientist.

"Why isn't Lady Shelby involved? She's worked very hard on this production."

Once again all eyes went every place. Most of them ended up on me.

"She has issues with me, Sir Devon," I said. "It goes back to last year at school."

"Kylie tried to include her, honest," Ophelia said.

"I have no doubt." He nodded the ponytail. "So she has chosen not to participate."

"Right," Tori said. "What's two?"

"It totally is," Ophelia said.

"But I would feel much better if you had someone behind you, spotting you."

I wasn't sure how that was going to help, but I didn't say anything. I was feeling really anxious, and I was afraid it would come out snarky.

"Let me speak with Lady Shelby," Sir Devon said. "Perhaps I can persuade her to take the job."

"She'll hate that idea," I said to Tori after he walked away.

Tori twisted her mouth. "Right now she kind of hates everything. I don't know what's going on with her." She shot me a look with those little bird eyes. "And it's not your fault, so don't even go there."

"Okay," I said.

∿

The show was performed at almost dusk on Saturday, so there was enough light to get around, but the twinkly lights the production crew put in the trees showed up like tiny fairies who had come to see. I could feel the specialness of the whole thing on my skin as people started arriving. Mom. Jocelyn. Even Mrs. Yeats—without the gold vest but, of course, with the wiggling chins.

I left my bag backstage and was about to hurry to the dance studio to be with the Wee Dancers when I saw Mom wave to me to come to her. When I got there, she was talking to a woman in the next log row back who had long blonde curls and a way of looking straight down her nose that made me want to say, *Who died and left you in charge?* I didn't, of course.

"Kylie, this is Mrs. Kershaw," Mom said.

194

Before I could even form *Who the world is Mrs. Kershaw?* in my brain, the woman stuck out her hand and shook my mine so hard I could almost hear my finger bones cracking.

"So you're the famous Lady Kylie," she said. "Now, see, you're shorter than I pictured you. I guess because my daughter talks about you like you're larger than life."

I wasn't sure what that meant, and I definitely didn't know whom she was talking about. I must have looked pretty clueless because Blonde Lady laughed and said, "Oh, sorry. I'm Abby's mom. She's been talking about you since the very first day."

"Seriously?" I said. The very first day when she acted like I was invisible and I thought she was a little brat? *That* first day?

"I was telling your mother," Blonde Lady said, "Abby's whole attitude has changed this summer, and I think it's because of you."

I mumbled something that I hoped sounded like *thank you* and rushed out. This wasn't the time to get the whole thick-throat thing going again.

Milady and I put the finishing touches on the Wee Dancers in the studio before we led them through the back way to sit in their chairs behind the stage until it was time for them to go on. Ginger and Ophelia were back there too, reassuring their nervous actors and gluing on some of the scales that had chosen that time to fall off the dragon's costume.

Ten minutes before the show was supposed to start, Felicity started squirming in her seat and turning red, and I knew what was going on there. I took her hat off of her and wrapped my jacket around her so no one would see her costume as we hurried to the bathroom.

Ginger was in there too. "The princess had to go potty," she said. When Felicity went into a stall, Ginger whispered, "Can we talk outside?"

I followed her to the little porch, where she kept talking in a sandpapery whisper.

"Izzy's here."

"*What?*"

"Shhh!"

"You saw her?"

Ginger nodded. The tiny flower she'd tucked into her hair fell out, and she caught it in her hand.

"Where?" I said.

"She was walking from the parking lot when I was coming here."

I wanted to run back to the Gathering Place and look for her—because this couldn't be good. But Ginger was starting to sweat, and she was about to crush the flower. Any minute she was going to freak out, and I didn't exactly blame her. I wasn't far from that myself.

"Here," I said, taking the flower from her.

I pulled one of the bobby pins out of my shorts pocket that I had in case some little lady-in-waiting's hat wouldn't stay on and attached the flower to it.

"You want me to put it in for you?" I asked.

"Yes," she said.

I twisted a curl of her red hair and slid the bobby-pinned flower around it. Last spring, I did a makeover on Ginger, for all the wrong reasons. Everything was so different now.

We both breathed. And the princess emerged from the bathroom. And I could hear Felicity saying, "Lady Kylie? Are you here?"

"Don't worry about Izzy," I said to Ginger. "She probably just wants to take more pictures of me. She doesn't know it's over yet. I bet if Sir Devon sees her, he'll make her leave."

"Okay," Ginger said, and she swept the princess back to the Gathering Place.

I didn't have time to think about Izzy after that. The music for the opening was just starting as Felicity and I slipped into our seats behind the stage. Her little hand was so clammy I considered putting some of our chalk on it. But, really, what was being in a show without sweaty palms? Unless you were doing a pyramid—that was another thing entirely.

It was amazing how fast the show went even with the pauses for laughter and clapping from the audience. Before we knew it, it was time for the ladies-in-waiting to make their entrance. The only problem with being backstage was that I could only see them from the side. At least Sir Devon was having it recorded. Maybe I could watch it with Lydia.

"I'm scared," a little voice whispered. Felicity's little voice.

"It's okay," another one answered. "You'll do good."

Abby.

The trumpets sounded, and Abby led the line onto the stage. The giant "Aww!" we expected rose from the audience, so the music waited until that died down and my Wee Dancers had taken their places in front of the throne. And then . . . they were like fairy princesses themselves. Every move was just as they'd learned it, and their pliés and leaps were as in unison as a gaggle of six-year-olds was going to get. The best part was the final curtsy, with their scarf skirts spreading out like pretty wings. That got a *Bravo!* from the audience. Started by somebody in Ophelia's family, I was sure.

Yeah, *bravo* was my new favorite word.

When the Wee Dancers ran off the stage, hats askew, two of them leaped into my arms at the same time. It wasn't hard to recognize Felicity; she was a dripping sponge by then. Took me a minute, though, to realize Abby was clinging to my neck and giggling. I couldn't help myself. I giggled too.

After that, we only had five more minutes until the curtain call. I left the Wee Dancers with Milady Bernstein and went to meet the other assistant directors so we could get ready for our bow. Everybody was there, chalking up. Shelby stepped out of the shadows and said, "So what am I supposed to do?"

"You can still do a split in front if you want to," I said.

"No." She gathered her full lips into a knot. "Sir Devon said I'm supposed to be a spotter."

"I know he wouldn't mind—"

"I said no!"

"Shhh, you guys," Mitch said in not much of a whisper. Fortunately, the audience was already clapping and whistling for the ladies-in-waiting, who were the first to take bows.

"You took gymnastics," I whispered to Shelby. "Just stand behind us and steady anybody who looks like she's going to fall."

"Whatever," she said.

Ophelia grabbed Shelby's arm and whispered, "Run on stage with us."

"Now!" Tori said.

Sir Devon was saying something about, "Let us raise our voices in cheers for our assistant directors who have volunteered their time this summer to help these young ones . . ."

I didn't hear the rest. Mitch and Tori and Ophelia were already in place. Winnie and Ginger got into their positions in front. I was surprised that Tori suddenly looked like she was about to be sick. For a second, I thought she was going to cave, but she stayed strong and put her hand down for me to take. Thank goodness for the chalk because she was as clammy as Felicity.

I let go to put my hands up in a *V*, but I had to pull hard, as if we were stuck. The pulling jerked me backward, and I had to correct—because nobody had my back, for real. But I went too far forward. I was going to fall, and I couldn't stop it.

I did the only thing I could think of in that nanosecond. I landed in front of the pyramid, just missing Winnie and Ginger, and went into a split.

The audience went nuts. It was hard to keep a smile on my face, and as soon as I could, I got up and cartwheeled off. My hands felt like they wanted to stick to the stage. What in the world?

Once I was in the wing, I turned, expecting to see the rest of the girls following me. Nobody was moving. The audience kept cheering, although that was starting to fade. Sir Devon came out and said, "Thank you, ladies! Thank you, everyone!" But they still didn't move.

It took another whole minute before they pried themselves loose from one another and the stage floor. A minute is like eternity in front of an audience. I'd heard of milking it for that last cheer, but come *on.*

I didn't know for sure until they were all finally offstage that something was really wrong. Ophelia was waving her hands in the air, like usual, only not. Mitch was wiping her hands on the back of her shorts, and Tori was staring at her palms like she was trying to figure out what chalk was made of. Ginger looked whiter than Winnie, and Winnie herself put her hands up to her face and started to cry.

Almost right away the crying turned to screaming, so loud that I could tell the audience, already starting to break up, must have heard it too because they went silent.

"It's no big deal, Winnie," Ophelia said. "The audience thought it was fabulous, only why are my hands—"

"Wait," Tori said. "She's hurt."

"Help me!" Winnie screamed.

Mitch pried Winnie's hands from her face, just as Sir Devon arrived on the scene.

"What's happening back here?" he said.

"My eyes!" Winnie said. I thought. By that time it was hard to understand what she was saying.

"What's wrong with your eyes?" Sir Devon said.

"That stuff got in them!"

"What stuff?"

"The chalk?" Tori said.

She and Ophelia and Mitch and Ginger were around Winnie like a picket fence. Even Sir Devon had a tough time getting close enough to look at Winnie's eyes.

"We all had chalk on our hands so we wouldn't slip," Tori told him.

"Yeah, only there's something wrong with it." Mitch put up her palm. Lint from her shorts and even the paint from the stage floor were clumped on it.

"My hands got stuck to the floor!"

"I was stuck to Kylie!"

"I thought that chalk felt weird—"

I couldn't tell who was talking. The only voice that stood out was Shelby's. She looked right at me and pointed her finger into my chest.

"You put something in the chalk, didn't you? Spray glue or something, right?"

"No!"

Shelby whipped her head toward the group around Winnie. "I told you we couldn't trust her! She did that whole thing to make you look like idiots. And now look at Winnie!"

I actually couldn't stop looking at Winnie. Her eyes were already so puffy they were practically swollen shut, and the skin around them was redder than any shade her pale face had ever turned.

"We shall sort all of that out at another time," Sir Devon said. "Tori, go get Winnie's parents. Ophelia, fetch some wet paper towels.

Ginger, you and Mitch help Winnie to a chair. Shelby, bring me the chalk so we can tell the paramedics what we're dealing with."

Girls scattered like ants. There was an order for everyone, except me.

I wanted to scream as loud as Winnie, *I didn't do this!* More than that, I wanted to help. But everybody was scurrying all around, and it seemed as if they were trying not to look at me. It was like I was invisible, to everyone but Shelby.

"They should have listened to me," she said. "Nobody changes that much."

Chapter Twenty

What started out as the very best night of my life turned out to be the worst. Mom and Jocelyn came backstage to see what was taking me so long, and Sir Devon asked them to take me home. We passed the paramedics on our way out. Winnie was still crying, and Shelby was still accusing me with her eyes.

When we got almost to the car, Milady Bernstein caught up with us. By then I was in the middle of trying to explain to Mom and Jocelyn what was going on, and it was coming out jumbled.

"Kylie," Mrs. Bernstein said, "we need the chalk to show the paramedics."

"Do we need a lawyer?" Mom asked.

"Mom!" Jocelyn said.

"I left it backstage," I said. "I didn't have time to put it in my bag."

"Where backstage?" Milady asked. "We can't find it."

I told her where I left it, and then I watched her. Did *she* think I did it? After all that had happened, did she believe what Shelby was saying? I couldn't tell. She was holding herself tall like a ballerina, and her face was focused like all she could think about was Winnie.

"It's not there," she said. "But we'll keep looking around."

"I can help," I said.

But she shook her head. "I think we should keep you away for right now, Kylie. For your own sake."

"What does that even mean?" Jocelyn asked as we headed for the car.

Mom didn't answer, but her lips were tight in an old way.

"I'm scared for Winnie," I said. "What if she goes blind or something?"

Jocelyn opened the car door, and the light made a path right across her green eyes. "Did you put glue in the chalk?"

"No!"

"Then it's not your fault."

Was that all anybody cared about?

I had a hard time sleeping that night, even though Jocelyn put on a really boring old movie that was supposed make me sleepy but put her out first. When I did doze off, it was only to dream about all of the girls with no eyes, stuck to one another and the walls and everything but me. I woke up early in a sweat that Felicity couldn't even have competed with, and since I couldn't go back to sleep, I went down to the library and sat in my usual chair, wishing Lydia were there. I didn't know what to do.

Mom found me later and brought me some tea, only I didn't drink it because it couldn't be the same as Margaret's or Lydia's. But we did talk, Mom and I, about how someone could have messed up the chalk and why someone would do it. I told her what I'd been sitting there thinking since the sun was just coming up.

"I think it was Izzy," I said. "Ginger told me she saw her before the show."

"Did *you* see her?" Mom asked.

I shook my head.

"I wonder if anyone else did. I certainly didn't. We can ask Jocelyn."

"Even if anybody else did, unless they actually saw her spraying glue into the chalk, we can't prove she did it."

"And we don't even know if that's what happened. That's just what Shelby said."

At the same moment my eyes met Mom's, and we stared at each other.

"Could Shelby have—"

"No," I said. "She's a part of their group against bullying. She still hates me, but why would she do that to *them*?"

Mom shrugged. Her shoulders looked smaller and bonier than ever this morning, like she shrunk during the night. "Did you put powder on your hands?"

"I didn't need to. Mine were only sticky from Tori's and Ophelia's hands."

"Who else knew you were using chalk?"

Mom was sounding as lawyery as Dad, but it was calming me down, so I thought about it. "Just us. Unless somebody in the group told somebody else, but it doesn't make sense that somebody outside would do this. And nobody else was allowed backstage."

"It wouldn't have been one of the little kids playing a joke?"

"No way!"

"I'm just trying to cover all the bases."

Mom took a gulp of her coffee, and I decided I should at least take a sip of my tea. It wasn't *that* bad.

"If Izzy were there, I think I know why," she said. "I've been keeping up with this ridiculous Instagram thing, which has been petering out, by the way."

So Lydia was right about that.

"But there's a new picture on there today. It's blurry because whoever took it was obviously far away and then enlarged it. It's of you standing on some kind of little porch—"

The bathroom building.

"And it looks like you're pulling another girl's hair."

"Oh, my gosh, she's, like, stalking me!"

"So it *was* taken last night."

"I was just putting a flower in Ginger's hair."

"She or one of those other little minxes was there, then," Mom said. "Kylie, I really want to put your father on this." She put up her hand as I sat stiffer. "I know he doesn't get what you've been doing with Lydia this summer—or what I've been doing with her either—but this is where he shines. It just doesn't seem right that they should continue to get away with this."

"I don't care if he does anything about it or not!" I tried to rein in my voice. Talk about triggers. "I just want to find out if Winnie's okay, and I want to know who did this to her. She doesn't deserve it."

Mom curled her hand around my wrist. "And you don't deserve to be blamed."

I still didn't know what to do. But I didn't feel so alone, sitting there with Mom, drinking from mugs and listening to the clock tick.

Later that day, Sunday, Sir Devon finally called to tell us that Winnie was going to be okay. She was allergic to whatever adhesive—sticky stuff—was in the chalk, so it puffed up her eyes and her hands, but it didn't affect her eyesight.

"And what about this idea that Kylie put the glue in the chalk?" Mom said to him. "It is absolutely absurd."

I didn't hear what Sir Devon said, but I could tell from Mom's tight face that she didn't like the answer.

"Tomorrow doesn't work," Mom said. "My husband is out of town until the evening . . . Tuesday doesn't give him enough time to . . . fine. Tuesday at ten."

When she hung up, I had already gone down several roads. I was going to be taken to juvenile detention on Tuesday. I was officially being kicked out of school. I was going to appear before a judge . . .

"We're meeting with Mrs. Yeats Tuesday morning," Mom said. "To sort the whole thing out."

"Who's going to be there?" I asked.

"Apparently half of Grass Valley. We're meeting in the conference room."

Okay, so it wasn't juvie or a courtroom. But somehow it seemed even scarier.

∿

The time between then and Tuesday morning was the longest day and a half of my life. I did enough cartwheels and forward rolls in Jocelyn's suite to wear out the carpet, but it was the only way I could think. When I wasn't doing that, I was curled up on the bed sorting it out with Margaret while she gave me yellow blinks and purred.

Did I want to point out that the only person who could possibly have done it was Shelby? But that still didn't work. She was so attached to Tori and her group now that she wouldn't do something that went totally against what they stood for. Did she hate me that much?

Should I try to bring Izzy into it? Maybe somebody talked about our pyramid and the chalk in some public place and she heard about it? Or Heidi or Riannon did and they put her up to it? That was way too unlikely, even for a small town like ours.

And wouldn't that all sound like I wanted to get somebody else in trouble? Would they just think I'd been acting all summer and planned the whole thing to make them look stupid to get back at them once and for all? They seemed to think that already because nobody called me to say, "Hey, I know you didn't do it." None of the girls or Milady Bernstein or Sir Devon.

All of the good feelings I'd had the last few weeks were gone. I was back to being totally alone—me against the G.G.s.

I hadn't thought of them as the Goody-Goodies for a long time. I wanted to flush the thought down the toilet.

So I was *not* in a good place when Dad came home Monday night. Mom had already filled him in on the phone, so he wasn't exactly in a good place either.

He paced around the kitchen while Mom and I sat in the breakfast nook.

"I am so over this whole thing," he said. "A kid can't even play a practical joke without it going to the Supreme Court."

"This is a culmination of things, Zach," Mom said.

"It's a vendetta against my daughter, is what it is. They're determined to keep her out of that school no matter what we do." Dad came to us and slammed his hands on the table. "Fine."

What did that mean?

"We're still going to the meeting tomorrow morning," Mom said.

Of course we were. What were they talking about?

"Oh, you better believe we are," Dad said. "How much . . . stuff am I going to have to sit through?"

"Dad?" I said.

He looked at me as if I'd just snuck in.

"Could you guys just not yell in there, in the meeting?"

"Why would you even say that?"

"Because you're yelling now," Mom said.

We both looked at him. I watched his face flip through all kinds of expressions. Finally he laughed—*laughed*—and said, "Now I've got two of you on my case. I'm in a lot of trouble."

He kissed us each on the forehead. That didn't fix it. Not even a little bit.

Chapter Twenty-One

M om wasn't exaggerating all that much about half of Grass Valley being there for the meeting at the school. As we walked up the front steps of Gold Country Middle on that late-July day—just like we did on that June day about a lifetime ago—Tori and her mom and dad were already going in the front door, and I could see Winnie on the other side with a yellowed lady I figured must be her grandmother.

This time as I walked up those steps, I *was* nervous—so nervous my palms were sweaty and my mouth was dry and my stomach was squeezing until I almost couldn't breathe. I had never been that scared. Ever.

Dad was being all cheerful, acting like he totally had this handled. Mom whispered that I looked nice and ran her hand up and down the back of my Felicity-damp shirt. But when we walked into the conference room and I saw not only Tori and her parents and Winnie and her grandma, but also Ophelia, Ginger, and Mitch—all with at least one parent each—plus Mrs. Yeats and Milady Bernstein, I thought I actually might throw up.

I'm terrified.

I didn't need my wee voice to tell me that. In fact, I hadn't thought in that voice for a while. I hadn't needed to.

And I couldn't need to now. I could almost hear another voice saying, *Take off the mask.*

"I believe this is almost everybody," Mrs. Yeats said. "We're just missing Shelby and her parents."

"I need to be excused to the restroom," I said, and without waiting for anybody to give me permission, I ran down the seventh grade hall to the first girls' bathroom I came to.

I expected to throw up, but I didn't. Still, I had to put some cold water on my face, maybe *wipe* off the mask, or I wasn't going to be able to be in the room when Shelby convinced everybody I couldn't change.

"Are you feeling sick too?"

I jumped. Tori was standing there.

"It's a scientific fact that when adrenaline pumps through your body, it can cause stomach upset."

So could being accused of something you didn't do.

I waited for Tori to go into one of the stalls, but she leaned against the sink next to the one I was using.

"You didn't do it, did you?" she asked.

I watched in the mirror as I shook my head. "But I can't prove I didn't, and I can't prove who did."

"Neither can I. I tried. We all did."

"All?" I said to the back of her reflection.

"Me. Phee. Winnie. Ginger. Mitch."

"But not Shelby."

"Shelby's not talking to us."

I looked at her actual face. It was sagging.

"Why not?"

"I don't know. I guess because we wouldn't go, 'Yes, we think Kylie put glue in our chalk so we'd look stupid on stage.'" Tori shrugged. "She got mad and she hasn't talked to any of us since."

I felt a surge of hope. "Thanks—I mean that you don't believe her. Maybe she won't show up."

"She has to," Tori said. "Her parents are the ones who said we had to have this meeting or they were going to the school board. Well, actually, to be precise, they were already going to go to the board, but Mrs. Yeats said we should do this first."

"How do you *know* all this stuff?"

"My parents told me."

"Do *they* think I did it?"

"Who?"

"Your parents. Everybody's parents."

Tori twisted her mouth in that way she had. "The parents are pretty much sick of this whole thing."

"My dad is too."

"They want it done."

"So do I! I wish Lydia were here."

Tori tilted her head. "Lydia?"

"Yeah. We've been working together all summer. She's the reason I've changed so much. If she were here, she could tell them."

Tori blinked like she was trying to take that in. I expected her to ask me all kinds of questions about Lydia, but she didn't. She said, "So you have to tell them."

"What?"

"You have to tell them that you've changed. You have to stand up for yourself because now *you're* being bullied."

"I don't even know how to do that."

"Really? *Really?*"

Tori rolled her eyes. I'd never seen her do that before, and it almost made me laugh. She wasn't very good at it.

"You've been standing up for yourself this entire year," she said. "Only now you're actually innocent. So do what you do the best, but for good this time."

"That's what Lydia said."

Tori shrugged again. "Of course she did."

The bathroom door opened, and Tori's mother poked her head in. "We're waiting for you girls," she said, and she didn't look all that happy that I was talking to Tori. But Tori said, "Be right there, Mom."

The door closed, and Tori looked me in the eyes. "I'll be praying for you," she said.

I walked into the conference room behind Tori and her mom, and the place went totally quiet, like everybody was holding their breath at the same time.

Mrs. Yeats waited until we were seated, and then she said, "I hope this is the last meeting we have to have on this matter of bullying among this group of girls."

"Hear, hear, Mrs. Yeats," Dad said.

I wanted to smack him.

"Although Saturday night's incident didn't take place at a school-sponsored event, Mr. and Mrs. Ryan are disturbed enough that they brought it to my attention and asked that it be considered as part of my decision on recommending that Kylie be reinstated as a student here."

Dad raised a finger. "May I say something because this is actually all a moot point—"

"No, Mr. Steppe, you may not. I prefer to hear from Shelby first."

"Who's Shelby?" Dad murmured to Mom.

I wanted to die.

Mrs. Yeats nodded to Shelby, whose reddish-blonde hair was like a veil over the sides of her face as she looked at the table and said, "Nobody can change as much as Kylie pretended to this summer, and what happened Saturday night proves it. It was her chalk, and nobody else touched it except her before everybody put it on. She's been waiting for a chance to get back at Tori and the Tribelet, and she did it at the show so the whole town could see it."

"There is so much wrong with that reasoning I don't even know where to start," Dad said with a laugh in his voice.

"Mr. Steppe, please," Mrs. Yeats said. "This is not a courtroom, and you are not the district attorney."

Her chins were very still. Dad was in trouble. As in, he was about to be tossed out of there, and I wouldn't have minded that a bit. I knew my skin was red everywhere you could see and then some.

Dad sat back in his chair and said to Mom out of the side of his mouth, "What the heck's a Tribelet?"

Mom whispered something in his ear, and he got up and stood in the corner of the room, eyebrows folded over on themselves.

"You can certainly see where his daughter gets her attitude," Winnie's grandmother said.

Winnie whimpered. Mitch grunted. Ginger grabbed on to her dad's hand. The whole thing was about to collapse like our pyramid, until Mrs. Yeats said, "Ladies and gentlemen, let's set a good example for our children."

Grown-ups pushed air out of their noses and twiddled their fingers. I guessed you never got over being afraid of the principal. Mrs. Yeats turned to Shelby, chins jiggling again.

"I've asked you this in private, Shelby, but I want you to say it in front of the group. Did you actually *see* Kylie put glue in the chalk?"

Shelby shook her head.

"Excuse me?"

"No. But she probably did it at home."

"Do you have any proof that Kylie has been 'pretending to change' this summer?"

"No. Well, yes. It's been on Instagram."

Shelby's mom, who looked like a grown-up version of her with glasses, said, "Instagram? What were you doing on Instagram?"

"And what did you see on Instagram?" Mrs. Yeats asked.

Ophelia waved her arm, but her mom nudged it down. Mitch gave one loud grunt. Winnie was clearly biting back tears, and Ginger was shaking her head. Only Tori stayed calm as she looked at me. Translation: *Keep your cool; you'll get your turn.*

Mom was folding and unfolding her hands, and I knew she wanted to say something, but Mrs. Yeats said, "Shelby?"

Shelby was so red she could've hidden in a cranberry bog. "There are all these pictures of Kylie hugging a kid and underneath it has her saying she hates the kids and she's only doing it to get back into cheerleading."

Mrs. Yeats stroked a chin. "Kylie herself posted these pictures?"

"Of course she did."

"Careful now, Shelby . . ."

"Okay, I don't know. But her friend was taking the pictures the whole time."

"Which friend?"

"Izzy."

Mrs. Yeats looked at Mrs. Bernstein and then back at Shelby. "We'll get back to that issue if we need to. Right now, I think we need to hear from Kylie."

Shelby's dad looked like he was going to say something, but Mrs.

Yeats gave him one of those principal looks, and he sat back in his chair. Then she turned to me.

"Kylie, please take this opportunity to defend yourself against these charges."

"I can't," I said.

Everybody started whispering, and Mrs. Yeats clapped her hands for order just like she did in an assembly. The room got quiet again.

"I don't understand, Kylie," Mrs. Yeats said. "Do you mean you did—"

"No," I said. "I didn't do it. For once I'm innocent, right?" My throat was getting thick, but I pushed on. "It's just that I can't prove I didn't do it, and I can't prove who did. All I can do is tell you what's happened to me this summer." I tried to clear my throat. "First of all, I want to apologize . . ." I looked at Shelby, who stared at her lap. "To you, Shelby, because I was a terrible friend to you. I used you to do my dirty work, and I tried to get you to lie for me right in this room. I don't blame you for hating me, and I don't blame your parents for saying you could never have anything to do with me again. I get why you didn't want me in Tori's group—because you got there first. I really do get that, and I won't try to be part of it. I won't make you choose."

If everybody else was surprised, they couldn't be any more so than I was. Where did that even come from? Apparently, there was more because I kept talking.

"And Tori and all of you in the Tribelet thing . . ." I coughed again. "The whole last school year all the things I did to you were way out of line, and I'll never do them again. I'm really sorry. You were decent to me this summer, and you gave me the benefit of the doubt even though you didn't even know I was working with Lydia. You totally gave me a chance, and I would never and I will never do anything to hurt you ever again."

Something strange was happening—something not just in my throat but behind my eyes. I still kept going, though.

"Mrs. Yeats made me work with Lydia, and at first, I wasn't going to really do what she told me. I was just going to pretend so I could be a cheerleader again. Shelby was right about that at first. But then Lydia taught me about triggers and about taking off my mask and dealing with my own smudges before I criticized other people. And she taught me that there aren't any rivals—so that's why I didn't do anything to that chalk to make you look stupid. Maybe you moms and dads will never believe me, and I can't change that. I can only change me. And I did. I really did."

By then I knew what was happening in my throat and behind my eyes and on my cheeks. I was crying. Hard.

And have I mentioned that I never cry?

The room was quiet again. Milady Bernstein slid a box of tissues across the table to me, and I soaked one of them all the way through without making a sound.

"Ms. George," Mrs. Yeats said, "are you and Winnie satisfied with that?"

"I don't want Winnie to grow up being suspicious and hateful," Winnie's grandmother said. "So yes. I'll give her that."

"Mr. and Mrs. Ryan?"

Shelby's mom pushed her glasses up her nose with one finger. "It's clear Kylie has made some progress," she said, "but how long is this going to last? Can't she make a new start somewhere else so we don't have to worry about this anymore?"

"No." We all stared at Tori. "I mean, please, no." She looked at her dad, who nodded for her to go on. "We need Kylie here. There are still kids out there who are going to try to bully this year, and Kylie can show them that a person *can* change. She's a leader, and we need her help or this really *is* going to go on and on."

Mrs. Yeats looked at me. "What about it, Kylie? Are you willing to be part of our anti-bullying movement?"

I looked at Tori. She just looked back with her little bird eyes, and I translated.

"I think I already am," I said.

The chins wiggled, happily, I thought. Mrs. Yeats smoothed a hand over her gray helmet of hair and said, "Mr. and Mrs. Ryan, if you want to pursue this further with the school board, that is your privilege, but I am going to recommend that Kylie be reinstated as a student here." She ducked her head for a second. "I apologize to you, Mr. Devon and Mrs. Bernstein, for taking up your time by having you here. I thought we would need you as character witnesses, but Kylie showed us her own character rather well, I think."

"No worries, Mrs. Yeats," Sir Devon said with a flourish of his hand. "I would not have missed this for the world."

"Me either," Milady said. "Oh, and Kylie, let's talk about cheer-leading practice. I hope your calendar is clear."

If I'd smiled any bigger, the corners of my mouth would have reached my earlobes.

Shelby and her parents hurried out of the room, and she didn't look at me as she went. She would probably never look at me again, and I had to be okay with that. Every one of the Tribelet girls—so *that* was what they called themselves—smiled or grinned or grunted at me as they filed out with their parents. The moms and dads still looked, what do you call that? Skeptical? But that was okay too. Lydia said some wounds take a long time to heal.

The only people left were Mom and Dad and me, and I wasn't sure why we were hanging out. I guessed it was to thank Mrs. Yeats.

"I'm sorry I had to shut you down, Mr. Steppe," she said. "But I think you can see now why I handled things the way I did. You should be very proud of Kylie."

Mom nodded. She might actually be beaming.

Dad clapped a hand on my shoulder. "I guess it was good for her. I didn't want to say this in front of the whole group or we would have had a riot on our hands. Talk about wasting people's time . . ."

"I don't understand," Mrs. Yeats said.

Neither did I, but my stomach started to squeeze again.

"I've spent the last two months buttering up the headmaster at the Roseville Academy, and he's agreed to admit Kylie for the next school year. So, like I said, this whole thing was a moot point. Although I'm glad Kylie had her day in court—"

"Absolutely not."

I bit back the screams that were about to come out of my mouth—because this was a trigger I couldn't *help* pulling. It was Mom who said, *Absolutely not.* And she added, "Kylie will be attending Gold Country Middle School this year and the year after. We have both benefited from your program."

Dad looked like he wanted to tear a poster off a wall. Just like I had that day, when this first started. He had more self-control than I did, at least long enough for the three of us to get out of Mrs. Yeats' office and into the car. Then he exploded on Mom.

I sat back and closed my eyes, and I whispered a prayer. Maybe my first one ever.

"God, thank You for getting me out of the bullying business."

I had finally found my one-liner.

Chapter Twenty-Two

During the weeks before school started, I felt like my life had been remodeled just like our house, and I was now seeing how it was all going to come together.

Not all of the new look was good.

First of all, Dad decided he wasn't going to try to prove that Izzy and Riannon and Heidi were behind the Instagram campaign against me. That was probably because he blamed Lydia—whom he still referred to as Lynda—for making me not want to be his princess anymore. I thought that was pretty bad logic for a lawyer, especially when he said this was just stuff kids did and it would blow over.

Mom was furious about that. But, then, she was furious with him all the time those days. I could hear either muffled arguing behind their bedroom door or the silent ignoring all over the house. I decided the silence was louder.

That got even harder to deal with when Jocelyn left for college. I didn't get to go with Mom to take her to San Francisco because I had cheerleading practice, and besides that, I was sure I would cry. Ever since that day in Mrs. Yeats' office, I'd been doing a lot of crying. I guessed I'd been saving up the tears for five years, and they were all coming out at once.

So I cried anyway because just as Jocelyn was getting into the SUV, which was so stuffed there was barely room for her, she looked at me with her green eyes and said, "You're a better person than I will ever be." I spent the whole afternoon after cheerleading that day holding Margaret and missing my sister.

The one thing that made that easier was that I had moved into my new room by then. It felt like it was time to graduate from pink, so Mom and I decorated it in Gold Country school colors—gold and blue, the color of the Grass Valley sky. Most of the stuff on the walls was all about school spirit—like big fluffy pom-poms Jocelyn had made for me as a going-away present and the official squad photo.

But one big space on the wall I could see from my bed was dedicated to a poster I designed. Every morning when I woke up, every night before I went to sleep, and every time I curled up there with Margaret and my sketch pad, the Code for Respecting the Dignity of Every Human Being was in front of me. It had taken me all summer to understand it, and I didn't want to forget.

I definitely needed the reminder when Lydia told me that Heidi and Riannon would be back at Gold Country Middle because they passed summer school and because they did community service with the Rotary Club that their dads belonged to. *My* dad said that amounted to them serving beans at one of the club's barbecues, and when they got bored, they just went and hung out somewhere. How that showed they could care about other people was a mystery to me.

"Why was I ever friends with them?" I pretty much shouted at Lydia. Then I lowered my voice because we were at Peet's—a place where they served tea almost as good as Lydia's—and people were staring at me from over the tops of the coffee bean displays. "I can't believe I didn't see what they were like."

Lydia stirred her Lady Grey for a whole minute before she answered. "I think they were exactly who you wanted them to be."

I really hated it when she was right like that. Now I couldn't even be mad.

"What do I do when I see them at school?" I asked.

"The same thing Tori and the Tribelet did when they saw you at camp."

I was going to have to think about that and probably discuss it with Kitty Margaret, who was spending less time under the bed in the new room. Come to think of it, I was spending less time wishing I could get under there with her too.

Those were the hardest parts about having a new life. The good parts were mostly about still meeting with Lydia once a week—with Mom sometimes joining us—and practicing with the squad.

That included me, Josie, and Brittney, who were from my section the past year in sixth grade, and three other girls who were in the other section and who I didn't know before we started spending every morning jumping over one another and building pyramids and sharing water bottles. Those were definitely the good times.

It was strange, though. Before that summer, when I thought the G.G.s were taking everything away from me (and I was wishing people would break out in severe acne), I used to assume that I would be a cheerleader and have the dreams come true that I'd been seeing in my mind almost my whole life. Now that I had it, two things were happening.

One, I didn't take it for granted anymore. I had to work for it just like everyone else. And I had never thought of myself as "like everyone else." I kind of liked it.

And two, I figured out cheerleading wasn't the only thing I

wanted. Okay, yeah, it was huge. But I also wanted to draw and be an assistant teacher at the dance studio where Milady Bernstein volunteered and—weirdest of all—be part of the Tribelet. Not as friends. We were still way too different for that. I mean, I couldn't relate to science and drama club and all that. But as a member of the bullying-is-so-not-okay thing.

I met with them a couple of times, but it was still what Attitude Abby would call "funky" because of Shelby. Tori said she always asked if I was going to be there so she'd know whether to come. Sometimes I didn't go so she could go.

But there was one thing I could do to help, and when I suggested it to Milady Bernstein and the squad, they were all over it. We created it together and choreographed our routine around it and practiced it in front of Mrs. Yeats and Mr. Malone, the new vice principal for the seventh grade. He was young and had dimples and wore Disney ties, which made me wonder if he was related to Felicity. I had a feeling the seventh grade was going to put him through the blender, but I was excited when he clapped for us until the palms of his hands were red.

Still, on the first day of school, when I once again climbed the front steps of Gold Country Middle, I was stomach-squeezing nervous again. Everything was different. Different friends. Different place in the class, as in, not the princess anymore. Different attitude.

∾

Some things were, however, the same.

Andrew and Patrick and Douglas were back on the front steps, spitting the same rude comments out of the corners of their mouths like sunflower seed shells. Why had I thought they were cute?

Even Douglas. Especially Douglas. It wasn't that I was off boys. Are you serious? I just didn't like *those* boys.

Heidi and Riannon and Izzy were in front of the trophy case in the front hall, so wrapped up in whatever they were planning they didn't seem to even notice me as I hurried past. It occurred to me that the posse was shrinking. Maybe someday it would disappear altogether, when the rest of them finally got it.

The first warning bell rang, and I headed straight for the gym where all the seventh graders were meeting for the opening assembly. One thing was definitely the same: as I got closer, I could smell the stinky tennis shoes and the boys who didn't get the whole deodorant thing. It wasn't all that comforting.

I was almost there, just passing the girls' restroom, when the door opened and Shelby stepped out into the hall, right in front of me. The crowd was getting thick, so there was no way for either one of us to escape. We could only stand there staring at each other, the way little kids do before they get manners.

I tried to find mine.

"Hi, Shelby," I said.

She mumbled something. It might have been 'Hi, Kylie,' but I wasn't sure because she was barely opening her mouth.

Then we stared at each other again, and that's when I saw that she wasn't looking so good. Her pale blue eyes were road-mapped with red lines, and the skin around them was puffy like she'd been doing a lot of crying. I knew the look from my own mirror.

"Are you okay?" I said.

She shrugged, and then she said, "No."

Clearly she was about to start bawling again right there, with Douglas and his pack just a few feet away, telling Riannon in raspy voices that she was a babe. I tugged at Shelby's sleeve and pulled her back into the restroom, which thankfully was empty. I checked under the stalls just to make sure, and when I turned back to Shelby, she was, just like I thought, crying again. And I didn't want to be the cause of anybody's crying anymore.

"Okay, here's the thing," I said. "Obviously, we can't both be in the Tribelet, so you go ahead and be part of it and I'll find other ways to help—"

"That's not why I don't go to the meetings if you're going to be there."

That came out between choky little sobs. I ripped a paper towel out of the dispenser and handed it to her and waited while she blew her nose.

"That's not why," she said again.

"Then . . . I don't get it," I said.

"I can't because . . ."

More tears. More nose-blowing. The final warning bell rang, which meant the assembly was going to start in five minutes. Shelby started for the door, but I caught her sleeve again.

"If I did something to hurt your feelings, dish, okay? I'm trying really hard to stay changed, but I know I can still be snark—"

"I'm afraid!"

I could feel my insides sinking. "Of me?"

"Of you telling them."

"Telling them . . ."

"That when you did the pyramid at camp, I didn't catch you when started to fall. And that I—"

I put up my hand, almost the way I used to when I was her bully. Only this time, I wanted it to be used for good.

"Are you sorry?" I said.

"Oh, Kylie, yes!" she said and put both hands over her face and cried so loud the sound echoed all around the bathroom.

"Then let's move on," I said above the wailing. "Okay?"

She nodded, still sobbing into her palms.

"I have to go," I said.

Shelby nodded again, and I raced for the gym. My feet felt light because that last piece was no longer dragging me down. I couldn't wait to tell Lydia. And Margaret. They were the only ones who had to know who put the glue in the chalk.

When I joined the other cheerleaders behind the first set of bleachers, Josie looked like she was going to evaporate with relief.

"We thought you weren't coming!"

"Are you serious?" I said.

"We're glad you made it, and you all look great," Milady Bernstein said. I didn't call her that out loud, but she would be called that name in my head forever.

Now that I was standing there with the squad, I could breathe and notice. The cheerleading uniform felt just the way I thought it would. Probably better. Even without the Jacket. I straightened my sweater and shook out my hair and checked the pleats in my skirt and generally just looked like I needed to make a trip back to the girls' restroom. Because now I was nervous all over again.

"Are you freaking out or something?" Josie said.

"No," I said. "Okay, yes."

"Why?" Brittney said. "The cheer's awesome, and we have it so down."

I knew that. I did. But there were a whole lot of people out there who might not think so. Those were the people who'd had me practically clutching my belly as I walked up those front steps.

And do you have any control over that?

That was Lydia's voice in my mind. My stomach stopped squeezing. Because when had she ever been wrong with me?

So even after Mrs. Yeats introduced Mr. Malone in his Mickey

Mouse tie—and he couldn't get the crowd calmed down; even after a whole row of seventh grade boys—led by Douglas—shouted out stuff like "This ain't kindergarten, man!" until Coach Zabriski marched three of them out, Patrick, Andrew, *and* Douglas; even after I heard Riannon yawn loudly enough for the whole gym to hear and say, "BO-ring"; even after all that, as soon as young Mr. Malone introduced us and we cartwheeled our way out onto the gym floor, I didn't care whether they were cheering or booing or snorting.

All I could think about was whether they were going to get what I'd convinced the squad we needed to say to them on this first day of school.

The gym did get quiet as we got into formation. Out of the silence someone yelled, "Go, Ky-LEE!" and other voices joined Tori's. With a smile as big as Lydia's watermelon slice, I stepped forward and said, "Ready? Okay!"

And then with our dance steps and our hand movements and finally our pyramid, we told them to the rhythm of clap, clap, stomp, stomp, stomp:

> *We are the Miners,*
> *The gold, blue, and white.*
> *It's a bully-free zone,*
> *So let's unite.*
> *Let's make a pact,*
> *A promise today:*
> *Bullying in 'the Country'*
> *Is SO not okay!*
> *Let's shout it out:*
> *SO not okay!*
> *Let us hear ya now*

SO not okay!

The second time around it seemed like all students were on their feet, stomping and clapping and yelling with us, "SO not okay!" They rocked the gym. I couldn't see Riannon or Heidi or Izzy, but I wasn't looking for them. I searched for Tori again, and I found her and I grinned right at her.

Translation: *I have left the bullying business for good. And I am SO okay.*

Who Helped Me Write
Sorry I'm Not Sorry

It takes more than just the author (me!) to write a book. These are the people who helped me get Kylie and the Tribelet's story as right as it can be:

Mary Lois Rue, who let me stay with her in Grass Valley and made it come alive for me. She's my mother-in-law, the other Mrs. Rue.

Amy and John Imel, my brother-in-law and sister-in-law who told me what it was like to grow up in Grass Valley, California. (And fed me wonderful food . . .)

My editors, **Molly Hodgin** and **Amy Kerr**, who caught all my mistakes and saved me from being totally embarrassed.

All the people who have written books and made films about the problem of bullying. And all the bloggers and website folks who kept me up to date. We call them the **SNOGS** (SO Not Okay Group Support)!

The **Mini-Women on the 'Tween, You and Me blog** who bravely shared their stories with me. They're the ones who showed me that "sticks and stones can break your bones, but words can break your heart." Come join us by clicking on the 'Tween You and Me blog on my website: **www.nancyrue.com**.

And especially Coach Hope Culver and the cheerleaders at Oakland Middle School in Murfreesboro, Tennessee, who created the cheer for Kylie:

Anna

Riley

Kya

Spencer

Maggie

Brooke

Kiley

Chloe

Haylie

Taylor

Wyn

Lauren

Sorry I'm Not Sorry is only one of three books that will make up the **Mean Girl Makeover** trilogy. If you would like to help with the last book by sharing your story of being the victim of bullying or your experience as a bully, please e-mail me at **nnrue@att.net**.

You can also be part of the solution by joining the So Not Okay Anti-Bullying Movement. Just go to **www.sonotokay.com**.

Blessings,
Nancy Rue

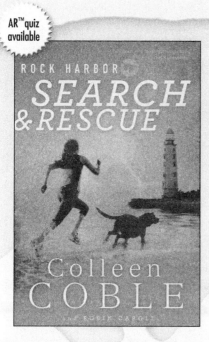

ROCK HARBOR

SEARCH & RESCUE

Colleen COBLE

FROM AWARD-WINNING AUTHOR COLLEEN COBLE COMES HER FIRST SERIES FOR YOUNG ADVENTURERS: A MIXTURE OF MYSTERY, SUSPENSE, ACTION—AND ADORABLE PUPPIES!

Eighth-grader Emily O'Reilly is obsessed with all things Search-and-Rescue. The almost-fourteen-year-old spends every spare moment on rescues with her stepmom Naomi and her canine partner Charley. But when an expensive necklace from a renowned jewelry artist is stolen under her care at the fall festival, Emily is determined to prove her innocence to a town that has immediately labeled her guilty.

As Emily sets out to restore her reputation, she isn't prepared for the surprises she and the Search-and-Rescue dogs uncover along the way. Will Emily ever find the real thief?

BY COLLEEN COBLE

www.tommynelson.com

www.colleencoble.com

9781400321995-B

If it is such a good thing, why does the Mark seem so wrong?

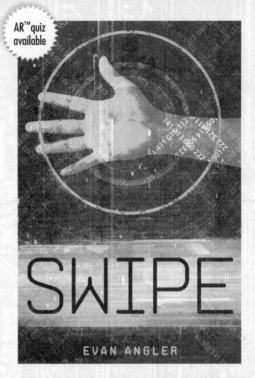

AR™ quiz available

SWIPE

EVAN ANGLER

Logan Langly is just months away from his thirteenth birthday, the day he will finally be Marked. The Mark lets people get jobs, vote, even go out to eat or buy concert tickets. But Logan can't shake the feeling he's being watched . . . and then he finds the wire.

By Evan Angler

www.tommynelson.com

www.evanangler.com

Look for more Swipe books coming soon!

SAVING THE WORLD
ONE DREAM AT A TIME

Fourteen-year-old Archer Keaton is a dreamtreader, one of three people in the entire world destined to defeat evil forces in the Dream World by using the power of imagination. The dreamtreaders are working to stop the Nightmare Lord, who terrorizes the dreams of innocent people all over the world. But as Archer's adventures in the Dream World become more threatening, so too does his waking life.

As Archer faces two foes in two worlds, will he be able to quell the nightmares haunting his dreams and reality?

THOMAS NELSON
Since 1798

AVAILABLE IN PRINT AND E-BOOK

A WHOLE NEW WORLD
FOR TWEEN READERS
TO EXPLORE!

Get lost in The Mysteries of Middlefield with Amish adventurers Mary Beth and Rebekah as they discover the danger and excitement of solving a good mystery.

By Amish fiction bestseller Kathleen Fuller
www.tommynelson.com

Look for book three, Hide and Secret *in Summer 2011.*